LEARNING SEASON

BLAINE R. SMITH

outskirts
press

PROLOGUE

The heavy, powerful staccato beat of the Apache attack helicopter's powerful engine always got Major James Douglas pumped. The machine he flew was, in his estimation, finely tuned for combat. It carried its full load of rockets and the pilot helmet-aimed 50 caliber machine gun. Even now, as he and his co-pilot sped toward danger to relieve the ambushed American base patrol he was confident, sure that his bird could handle any enemy threat. As much as he missed his wife and two kids, he grudgingly had to admit to himself, he was born to do the job he was doing – flying an attack helicopter into battle. 'I hope they're OK,' he thought to himself as he pushed his stick farther over with his right hand and increased the torque to gain more speed, 'I sure wish I could get home to see them.' His headphones crackled to life with his copilot's voice jerking his mind forcefully to the business at hand. He adjusted the volume with his left hand.

"I think I see blue smoke off to the right major."

"Roger. I see it. I think I see enemy mortar pits in those rocks just off to the left there!"

"Whiskey One Niner," the base communications spec called out his helicopter ID, W – 19. "Do you copy?"

"Roger," James answered. "This is Apache Attack One Niner. Request heading information. . . ."

"Whiskey One Niner take angels 140 from current heading. Enemy targets two klicks. Alpha Patrol should be on your immediate right along the mountain side. Alpha Patrol will throw blue smoke. Say again, blue smoke."

"Roger base. Have blue smoke in sight at 10 degrees at the mountain's base. Turning toward enemy targets. Request permission to engage."

"Roger One Niner. You have permission to engage."

"Whiskey One Niner, this is Colonel Smith. JD, you've got to be careful. They've got Syrian shoulder mounted ground to air missiles, the MANPADS, and also the FIM 92 Stingers. We found some in a cache we discovered last week. Don't get too close!"

"Copy that Colonel. The patrol is taking heavy mortar fire. We've got to get down there and help or they won't last 5 more minutes!"

"Just be careful for God's sake! Don't push the envelope."

James pushed the nose of the copter over and swooped in on the enemy position. He triggered the 50 caliber belly mounted machine gun and watched it rip the ground around the mortar pits. Swinging the rotor he turned the copter and let loose four rockets at the nearest line of enemy who were firing on the American patrol below. At least 25 of the enemy disappeared in the explosions as the rockets impacted. He was almost in awe of the destructive power he wielded.

"Pull up major!" his copilot screamed in his ear as he swooped even lower to engage an ISIS machine gun nest on the mountainside. "We're too low. We're sitting ducks!"

"Steady Ray. We've got to give that patrol time to clear out of there!"

The metallic plunk, plunk, and rrrrring told James that enemy rifle fire was impacting the helo. An AK-47 round broke through the Apache's windshield and tore into the ceiling of the cockpit.

"Jesus!" said Ray. "That was close!" The engine oil pressure alarm began chiming loudly.

"We're losing oil pressure Major, we gotta get outa here!"

"Damn, must've taken a hit in the engine; how's that patrol?"

"Looks like they've cleared the ridge major. Let's get out of here!"

"OK Ray, it's getting a little warm, maybe we better go cool off huh?" James deadpanned as he jerked the stick hard right to exit the combat zone. Wham! The concussion from the impacting Stinger missile almost knocked him out. In one instant the main data display board was alive with screaming alarms, and he had almost zero stabilization control. His Apache was beginning to twist violently in a tight downward spiral.

"Apache Base. This is Whiskey One Niner....we're hit. Say again. . .hit. . .enemy missile. . .trying. . .regain control. . .not. . . make base. . . rescue one! Say again, launch rescue . . . one! " James barked into his mouthpiece as he fought his increasingly unresponsive craft.

"Ray, engage the fire suppression system!" he screamed. "Ray!" As he fought the controls he managed a glance at his unconscious, fatally wounded copilot, blood spurting from a deep slash in his throat. It was then that James noticed the blood pouring out of the horrific gash in his own right side, soaking his flight suit. Pain registered then. Sharp, gut wrenching pain. Pain that his mind tried to set aside. He had no time for that. He coughed, suddenly aware he was unable to gain a breath. He willed himself to ignore that also, no time for that either. But the pain returned, intense pain; so intense it made him nauseous. He coughed again, trying in vain to get some air, but the coughing caused more pain. Blood filled his mouth, then dribbled down his chin; it filled his throat and caused him to gag. He tried vainly to spit it out, and felt more pain. He involuntarily tried to take a deep breath, and waves of pain that nearly made him pass out, hit him. Choking on more blood, he coughed again, which caused excruciating pain to shoot through his chest, and more blood to pour out of his side and run out of his mouth. Through sheer will he forced his mind back to his bird.

The copter heaved up, then down, twisted, and flailed in the sky, a wounded bird dropping to the ground. Using all his 18 years of helicopter flight experience Major James Douglas momentarily righted the Apache into a level attitude. A brief moment of hope surged through him as he thought he might be able to save it, only to disappear as his dying Apache nosed over and continued its twisting plunge earthward. He could not stop it. He had lost all control; all flight dynamics were gone.

"I'm not going to make it," he thought out loud. The realization shocked him. The finality of it filled him with intense, overwhelming sadness and regret. The ground rushed towards his cockpit window. In those last seconds the faces of his wife, son and little daughter filled his mind. "Honey...kids...no..." he whispered to himself, unaware that base camp heard every word. "God.... Oh. . . . "

"Noooo!!" John Douglas screamed as he jerked awake, sweat drops running down his face. His chest heaved up and down as he tried to get air. The dream had come again. The dream, when it came, was always the same. The dream never changed. It was a dream of his father, Major James Douglas, flying his US Army Apache. It haunted him. It made him fear sleep. He did not want to dream the dream; it came of its own volition. Against his will, the dream forced itself upon him, the result of the love he felt for his father and his subconscious struggling to deal with the information the US Army had provided to the young man's family about his father's last flight. The dream was always the same, always. "Dad," he whispered to the darkness, as a large, single tear slowly wound its way down his cheek. cheek. "Dad. . . no . . . no . . ." he whispered involuntarily. He laid his head back on his pillow and rolled, facing the wall. He felt his worried mother's hand gently rub his back and the troubled young man slowly relaxed into a light slumber.

CHAPTER 1

The next afternoon as John Douglas half strolled, half jogged onto the warm, dusty practice field his coach's anger grew and by the time John reached the group of scrimmaging players the coach had lost his patience.

"Douglas!" he said stridently, "you're going to run four extra laps after practice! Can't you get here on time!? There's 25 other players here on time! What? Do you think you're special?"

John didn't say anything, but the fact was, he DID think he was special. Even though he was only a junior, he knew no one on the team was as quick or could throw as well as he could. At 6'1", and 185 pounds, John was the key to the team's league title hopes and he knew it. He wasn't very happy about running four extra laps; after all, on this practice field, that was one mile. 'Well,' he thought, 'maybe I can talk coach out of it later.'

John warmed up his legs and stretched his muscles on the side while his team continued to run through the offense. The first game was only 3 days away, and coach Mac was nervous. After about 15 minutes of warming up, John approached coach Mac.

"Ready to go, coach," said John, trying to be friendly.

"Go where?" coach Mac asked, coldly.

'Geez,' he thought to himself, 'What is coach's problem? He knows I'm the best quarterback and he knows he needs me.'

"Well," John said, "I thought I should run some plays with the . . . ." He stopped, seeing the anger in his coach's eyes. Then offered plaintively, "There is a game Friday."

"Oh, YOU thought you should run some plays, Huh? Well, let me clue you in, Mr. Douglas, I decide who does what on this team. You're on second team!"

John was startled, almost shocked. He had not expected this. He numbly stepped back behind the first group, wanting to disappear. As he stood in line behind the first offense, he heard some of his teammates quietly agreeing with what the coach had done. His anger rose. As he continued to hear the quiet "it's about time", "good, he's always late" comments from the other second stringers his wrath increased.Finally he couldn't stand the humiliation any longer.

He spun around and yelled, "What's wrong with you losers, don't you want to win Friday?"

"That's enough Douglas," said coach Mac, "you run your laps now and get to the showers! Maybe you can come back with a better attitude tomorrow."

John wheeled around facing coach Mac, but stifled his urge to scream at his coach. Even though he thought he was being unfairly treated he still wanted to play football. In fact, he had wanted to play varsity football as long as he remembered. He had grown up looking at his dad's football trophies, playing catch with his dad, and talking sports with his dad. His dad had always helped and encouraged him to play sports. He had to stay on the team. He slammed his helmet down on his head and angrily stomped off on his laps, calling the second stringers "losers" under his breath again as he passed them.

Coach Mac watched him run off with a mixture of disgust and grudging admiration. Even jogging, the young man's fluid, easy stride showed his athleticism. Mac knew he needed that kid in the game. But, not with his attitude. The kid had to learn.

He turned his attention back to the team. They were running the plays crisply and Bobby was doing a good job at quarterback. He wasn't as fast as John, nor did he have as good an arm, but his teammates rallied behind him, and that was important.

After another 45 minutes of offense coach Mac called the team together. "OK men, we had a good practice today. Tomorrow we are going over the defense." At this the more aggressive players shouted joyously. "Hold it down, hold it down, you'll get your chance tomorrow. Now, let's run 16 forty yard sprints!" A remark met with 25 players moaning as one. "Hey, we gotta be in shape men!" said coach Mac. He then directed his two assistants to take care of the sprints and walked toward his small office in the corner of the gymnasium thinking about Douglas as he went.

The game Friday was not a league game, nevertheless, without John in the game the team was weaker on offense and especially weak on defense. The kid had such talent, and only a junior! He was still growing and would be even bigger next year. He could hear John showering when he went in his old, musty, varsity coach's office. He decided against talking to him again. Mac knew John's attitude had to change or the team wouldn't follow him. What he didn't know was how to change it. He inhaled and let out a long sigh, if he didn't win some games this year, he might not be coaching next year. This was supposed to be fun, he thought, as he sat down to go over some defensive formations. He figured he had another hour of work to go before he got home.

Still mad when he walked in the kitchen door, John slammed his books down on the table and looked in the refrigerator for a snack. He was munching on a candy bar and drinking some milk when his little sister Mary came running in.

"Can I have a bite?" she said.

"No! This is mine, go away."

"Why can't I have a bite? You're mean, I'm telling Mom!"

"Go ahead, you ugly twerp," John said as his sister ran off crying.

"You shouldn't treat your sister that way," John's mom said as she walked in.

"Mom, she bugs! She won't leave me alone. She wants my food, she's always wanting attention. Geeez!"

"Well, she does love you. I think you should try to love her back. She's the only sister you have." Mrs. Douglas eyed her son thoughtfully then said, " So.... how did practice go today?"

"First coach and now you! I don't know if I can handle coach on my back much longer."

"What happened? Did you do something?"

"Just because I was 15 minutes late to practice, coach put me on the second string, then he made me run an extra mile and sent me home!" John knew he was leaving out a few details, but he didn't care. "I don't get it. I'm the best quarterback, everyone on the team knows it!"

"Why were you late, did you have to see a teacher after school?"

John didn't know how to answer that. He decided to avoid it. "I'm going to go do some homework," he said as he walked down the hall to his room, where he didn't do any homework at all.

John's mom was puzzled. 'He is so hard to get along with sometimes, even more so this past year,' she thought, 'He used to be so nice. Ever since his father . . .' She let the thought dangle in her mind. She sighed, "Sometimes I don't know what to do with him," she said to the empty kitchen.

Around 7:30 in the evening the doorbell rang. Mrs. Douglas opened the door to see Skip (short for Skipper) Wilson and Pete (short for Pedro) Silva standing there. "Come in boys," she said, "John's in his room." She was glad they were here, they were John's best friends on the team. As the boys walked down the hall she had a thought. "Skipper, can you come here for a minute?" she asked.

When he stood before her and she asked him quietly why John had been late to practice, Skip squirmed. She knew she had put him on the spot. "Skipper, John took it very hard when his father didn't return from Iraq, and now there's only me and his sister. I just want to try to help him, but sometimes I don't know what to do."

"Well, I probably shouldn't say, but he's been staying in the gym talking to a girl named Wendy before volleyball practice. That doesn't start until 3:30 and our practice starts at 3:15 sharp. You know coach Mac." He shrugged his shoulders, "I told him not to, that coach Mac wouldn't like it, but he does it anyway."

"Thanks Skipper, that's all I wanted. Don't worry, I won't tell him you told me."

"Thanks Mrs. Douglas," Skip sighed, relieved.

John and Pete came bouncing down the hall. It's nice to see him smile, thought Mrs. Douglas, he doesn't do that much anymore.

"Mom, we thought we would go down and get a hamburger. OK?"

"Well, I don't know, it is a school night. Maybe you better stay here."

"Maaaaawm! Come on!" John whined.

"Lighten up John," said Skip, "How about if we promise to have JD back by 8:30 Mrs. Douglas?" Skipper smiled, his white teeth showing bright against his black skin.

Mrs. Douglas considered for a moment. She usually didn't let John go out on school nights, and she really didn't have the money for this sort of thing, but she had a feeling that it might be good for him to go with his two friends tonight. She dug in her purse for some bills for John, though she couldn't really afford it. "OK , but be back by 8:30."

As they left, she suddenly felt tired. She missed her husband terribly. She rested her head in her hands as she thought things out. Her son was becoming harder to handle. He was acting like he had the BIG head. She had grown up in Fort Sage and since they had been stationed here when the army sent her husband's squadron to Iraq, she thought it best to remain after the news about her husband. She had friends here. Mrs. Douglas decided to talk to her son in the morning about Wendy, then she called her daughter in to read a bedtime story.

The three boys took their burgers and fries outside the Fort Sage Burger Bonanza and sat at a table. A few cars drove up and down the short main drag that blinked with the lights of the few businesses of the small town. The September night was a little chilly, with a slight breeze blowing in off the high plains and the boys pulled on their royal blue and gold letter jackets with the large F/S on the front. Last year as sophomores all three had earned varsity letters. John, as a sometimes starter on the basketball team, Skipper, as a sprinter in track, and Pedro, as the catcher on the baseball team. They were probably the best junior athletes the school had been lucky to have in a long time.

As they ate, John watched the cars moving through the town's 3 stop lights. He liked this little place, he thought. He was glad his dad had been stationed here. Supported by ranchers and the nearby small army depot, it had most of the businesses one needed. There was a large Home Market with the best meat in town, Mr. Zendejas's Hardware and Nursery, a large Drug Store, a J.C. Penny store, a hospital, and an old drive-in movie theater. It only showed movies on Saturday nights now but that was OK. Rumor had it that a Walmart was in the works. He couldn't wait for the new ice cream parlor that was being built on Main Street to open up. He was mentally building his first giant banana split when Pete spoke.

"Man John, you sure ticked off coach Mac today."

"Hey, what do you know about it?" asked JD scornfully.

"Well, I know this much, if you keep showing up late to practice you won't be throwing me any touchdowns," said Skip, "in fact, you'll be off the team."

"You know coach won't kick me off. I'm too good.

He needs me. You watch, I'll be QB before the first quarter is over Friday."

Pete and Skipper rolled their eyes at each other. They had seen John act like this more and more often. It bothered both of them. The boys ate their 1/2 pound burgers in silence. As they started on their jumbo fry baskets Pete said, "John, some of the things you've been saying have really turned some people off."

"Like what? Some people would be better off keeping their nose out of my business."

"Like calling the second string 'losers'," interjected Skipper. "You didn't have to do that. The guys on the team won't follow you, JD, if you do things like that."

"Pffft. I don't need them! Just give me the ball, and I'll take care of the rest."

"Well, Pete and I think it's something you better think about." Skipper looked at his watch, "Come on guys, it's 8:25 and we promised we be back by 8:30." Just then Wendy drove up in her dad's midnight blue, 65 Mustang and parked on the curb. Wendy was a cute little girl with a ton of energy that played 'setter' on the school volleyball team. She wore her brunette hair short, in a Dorothy Hammill cut, and her blue eyes sparkled in the light as she leaned over to talk to the boys.

"You and Pete go ahead, I'll ride with Wendy," said John.

Skip and Pete watched him walk over to the car to talk to Wendy. "Come on Skip, let's go," said Pete.

"No way, I told his mother I'd have him back at 8:30 and that's just what I'm going to do," Skip said forcefully as he walked up to Wendy's side of the car.

"Hi Wendy, sorry to break this up, but I've got to take JD home."

"Oh, gee, don't be a party pooper. I can take him," said Wendy smiling.

"Nope, I can't let you do that. I told his mom I'd bring him back by 8:30. Come on JD."

"Get out of here Skipper!" said JD loudly, gesturing with his right hand. "You're not my dad!"

The remark made Skipper feel a deep sympathy for his friend. Nevertheless, he had made a promise to JD's mom. He reached in and grabbed the keys. "No one's going anywhere until JD gets in my car. And I'm prepared to sit here until Wendy's dad comes looking for her. Don't try to come get them. You think you're faster than me, but I guarantee you, you're not."

Irritated as he was, John knew Skipper had him. Skip was the one player on the team that had the same speed as him in the 40 yard dash.

"OK, OK, I'm going. See you tomorrow at school Wendy."

"Bye JD," said Wendy as he left. Then she turned to Skipper, "Why did you do that? I would have taken him right home."

"I know that, but I told his mother I was going to do something, and I intend to keep my word. We're trying to help JD out, why don't you?"

"What's that supposed to mean?"

"It means, if you really like him, you'll quit making him late to practice," said Skip as he walked off.

Wendy blushed. She didn't think she had caused John trouble by talking to him in the gym, at least, he had told her not to worry.

As Skipper pulled up to the driveway John said, "Hey, thanks for ruining my evening guys. Someday I'll return the favor."

"Look, I didn't want to do that," said Skip, "But I had made a promise to your mom. Now, let me get out and apologize to her for getting back 5 minutes late."

"Think we did any good?" asked Pedro as Skip returned to the car. Skip shook his head as he pulled the car away. "I don't know. . . .I just don't know."

CHAPTER 2

C oach MacDonald opened the door to his dusty, little office at 6:30 the next morning. It was Wednesday and the team would be going over defense in practice and he wanted to go over the depth chart before he had to start classes at 8:15. Over a cup of donut shop coffee he began to think things through. Fort Sage was a small town but they took their high school sports seriously. Every school they played had a larger student body, and Central Valley, their arch rivals, was twice as big. Still, a little more than 20 years back the teams from this little high school had won 3 state football championships in a row and dominated the league championships year after year. Mac himself had played on the last state championship team.

In a decision fraught with controversy the school board had named him head coach 2 years ago at the end of a season that saw the team lose every single game. Before that the team had managed 2 losing seasons in a row. Mac had been teaching and coaching sports at Fort Sage High for 10 years and had been one of the varsity assistants during those losing years. Although everyone in town agreed that the players loved him, that they would go through fire for him, there were some in town who had fought against his appointment because of his association with those losing teams. His team had won 2 of their 9 games his first year, and 3 last year. Mac felt they were making progress but they hadn't beaten hated Central Valley High either year and the 'victory bell', the golden prize that went to the game's winner, had remained at Central Valley for 5 straight years now. People in town were starting to grumble, some had even spoken up at the booster club meetings. The pressure was heating up.

He knew his team this year was young. They had lost 7 good seniors to army transfers and that left him with just 6 returning. Still, he felt he could have a good team. Offensively, he could use Bobby Garcia, a senior, at quarterback, if he needed him; two big 220 pound juniors at tackle in Robert and Scott; Josh, a senior at center and seniors at both guard slots - Smith and Reyes. His best offensive weapons were Wilson, probably the fastest receiver in the league, and Pedro Silva, the 'bull', at fullback. He usually used three or four formations, numbered his running backs' holes even to the right and odd to the left. Each back was numbered, making plays easier to call and execute.

For example, a 34 right, out of any formation, would mean Silva would take the ball through the four hole on the right side. Mac believed execution was a key to winning, so he didn't confuse his players with too many plays, formations or play names. He also used simple pass route terminology; he didn't want any confusion on the field. Defensively, he had always preferred the 5-2 alignment with a 'monster' back. The 'monster' acted like a roaming free safety, sometimes lining up on the other team's strong side, sometimes keying on their best runner.

The defense had been a strong point last year and

he had 3 all league selections returning. Bobby had been all league last year at cornerback, Josh, the center, had been an all-league linebacker, and big Paul, his last senior, an all-league defensive end. He had 5 juniors that were ready for the 'big time'. Wilson at safety, Silva at the other linebacker slot, big, quiet Scott at tackle, Robert Palcedo at the other tackle, and Douglas. But what the team needed most was for that Douglas kid to settle down. He could run and throw better than Bobby; he was quick, and a sure, aggressive tackler. He was clearly the best athlete on the team. Trouble was, the kid knew it. Looking at it all on paper, with a little luck, they could challenge for the league title this year. But next year, next year, well, that would be their year. Unfortunately, not all of the townspeople were looking at things the way he was.

At 7:45 Mac's two assistants, Keith Roberts and George Archer, entered the door looking glum.

"What happened guys? You both look like your dog ate your birthday cake," said Mac.

Keith spoke first. "We heard that a group of the so called town big shots got together last night at the Branding Iron Club to review the school's football team and coaches."

"And we were told that if this team didn't win the league and beat Central Valley this year the coaches are history," said George. "Don't they know we're working our tails off?"

Mac absorbed this latest news with his usual 'nothing bothers me look', but he could already feel his stomach tightening. He liked these two young men, even though they complained that he was inflexible and resistant to innovation. Both had played college ball, Keith as a center, and George as a tight end. They knew their stuff. He knew they wanted some reassurance. His problem was he knew that what they said was probably true.

"Look guys, I know some people in the town are after us. I grew up here so I know what can happen when this football team doesn't at least beat Central Valley every couple of years. All we can do is take this season one game at time. If we start worrying about what everyone is saying not only will we not be paying attention to football, but we'll all have ulcers by the end of the season. Now, have a donut, and let's go over defense before classes start." It sounded good, but Mac wasn't sure even he believed it.

That same morning, John's mom was sitting at the kitchen table drinking some hot apple cider when he came in for breakfast. "Would you like me to fix you some hot oatmeal?" she asked.

"No, that's alright. I think I'll just have some cold cereal and toast."

"John, have you been seeing a girl named Wendy?" asked his Mother, quietly. John was quiet. 'How had she found that out?' he wondered. Well, she didn't seem to mind. "Um, yeah, I have her in a couple of classes at school this year. I first met her last year in geometry class. We've met for lunch and stuff. We're sort of going together. How did you find out about her anyway?"

"Oh, you know us mothers, we find everything out," smiled Mrs. Douglas. "Why don't you bring her by one day so we can meet?" They were both silent for a while. Then Mrs. Douglas said quietly, "I wanted to talk to you about practice yesterday and your run-in with coach Mac. He and I went to high school together you know."

In fact, John hadn't known that. He stopped eating, expecting his mom to say more. When she didn't, he asked her why she wanted to talk about it.

Mrs. Douglas chose her words carefully. She didn't want to anger her son and she wanted him to listen to what she was trying to say. "It's just that, well, I've never found coach Mac to be unreasonable. I think you may have a way to go to college with your sports; there's no way I can pay for it now, since, well... your dad. But you've got to learn to listen to your coaches."

"Mom, I try, but coach is always picking on me!"

"That's what I'm talking about. I don't think coach would pick on you without a reason."

John finished his cereal and began gathering his books to leave. As he reached the door he turned, "Mom, coach always has to have things his way. He never listens to anyone. Just because I was a little late yesterday he put me down on second string. I don't think it is fair."

Mrs. Douglas followed him to the door and as he was walking down the driveway she called after him, "Maybe if you quit talking to Wendy in the gym and get to practice on time you and coach would get along better."

John turned and stared red faced. How in the heck did she find these things out? "Ah, OK Mom, I'll be there on time from now on. I'll see you later."

Mrs. Douglas smiled. Sometimes she could still see the 4 year old toddler in her 17 year old young man.

Later that day, John watched the clock click off another minute during his sixth period English class. His teacher was going on and on about the correct way to write a short essay and he was bored. He had fifteen more minutes and then he could see Wendy before practice. When the bell finally rang he wrote down the next week's reading assignment, gathered his books and went outside. He walked to the shaded lunch area where he had met Wendy the last few days after school. As he looked around for her in the laughing, milling crowd of students Pete and Skip walked up.

"Ready for practice John?"

"Yea, sure, Skipper. I'm going to wait for Wendy, then I'll come."

"Better get there on time today, we're going over the defense and you know coach won't like it if you're late again," said Pedro.

"Don't worry, I'll be on time Pete. Somehow my mom found out I'd been staying in the gym talking to Wendy before practice," said John as he looked suspiciously at Skipper.

"Man, those moms, you never know how they find stuff out!" laughed Skip. "We're going to go dress out. See you in the locker room."

John was becoming impatient. His glance hurried across the somewhat small campus, looking for her. Fort Sage High School housed roughly 800 students in its 2 two story and 5 single story buildings and one gym. It was really a very aesthetic campus, with green vines growing on up the red brick walls and flowers lining the walkways. Tall poplars, pine and ash trees dotted the open areas around the classrooms. The old, two-story buildings were the original elementary and secondary school buildings and each had balconies surrounding the upstairs classrooms. However, in his impatient state, JD failed to see the beauty in the school. His one overriding thought was, 'Where was Wendy?'

After about 2 more minutes he found her talking to Stan, a tall senior, over by her Spanish classroom. He stomped over to where they stood.

As he arrived Stan said goodbye and walked toward the gym.

"Hi JD!" bubbled Wendy as he walked up. "Whatcha doing?"

"Waiting for you!" barked John. "Been over there for 10 minutes! What're you doing talking to him?"

"Oh, we had to go over some stuff with Mrs. Garcia, that's all," said Wendy, surprised at his tone.

"Well, I don't like waiting for you and I don't like you talking to him."

"Well, excuse me! I'm sorry you had to wait. We had to clear up a Spanish assignment, and that's all. You don't have to get mad about it." Wendy looked at her watch. "I'm going to go to practice and I don't think you should come in to watch."

John, not understanding that she was trying to help him like Skipper had suggested, said, "Hey, fine with me, I wasn't planning on it anyway! I'm going to practice."

The hurt showed in Wendy's clear blue eyes as she said softly, "I'm only trying to make sure you're not late to practice. You don't have to talk to me like that. I'll see you tomorrow." Then she turned and walked off.

John didn't know what to do. He knew he had hurt Wendy's feelings, but he wasn't willing to apologize. Angrily, he went to dress out for his own practice.

Coach Mac called the team together after warm ups and began to explain the starting defensive alignments for the game that was now only 2 days away. He went over the defensive line and linebackers first. When he finally got to the defensive backs John was beside himself with anticipation.

"At left corner, we'll have Bobby, right corner Juan, you'll start at safety Wilson, and our monster back will be Douglas. Now I want that group lined up over the ball right now."

As John took his position he said quietly to Skip, "It's about time someone woke up around here. I should be starting at quarterback also."

Skip didn't have time to say anything because coach Mac was right in John's face. "Mr. Douglas, do you have any more comments!?" he shouted.

John had not meant for coach to hear and he knew he was in trouble now so he didn't say anything, but his anger rose at being singled out by the coach. 'This guy is always on my case,' he thought. "One more little comment from you, Mr. Douglas, about who plays where on this team, and you won't do anything but run water in during timeouts! Do you understand!?" yelled coach Mac.

"Yeah, I do," answered John angrily.

"That's good Douglas, because I've just about had it with your attitude," said coach Mac as he stomped off to begin explaining the defensive formations.

The defense spent 45 minutes scrimmaging against a not very willing second string offense that was running plays that the coaches thought would be used by Western High on Friday. The two assistants would show the offensive team diagrams of the Western plays and tell them how to run them, while coach Mac went over the blitzes and alignments the first defense would use. The scrimmage finally had to be called off because of the hard hits being administered by the defense. After they finished with defense the team spent a half hour reviewing offensive plays and extra point attempts. Finally, coach Mac blew his whistle and signaled the end of practice, called the team together, and had them take a knee in front of him.

"Now men, Friday we will play our first game, over there at Western. Even though they're not in our league, we want to beat them and get our season off on the right foot." At this the team cheered loudly. Coach held up his hands for quiet. "Now look, they've got two strong runners and a good quarterback this year, but we feel our defense can handle them. We've had 3 good weeks of practice. Our plan is to try to control the ball, score first and then clamp down on them with our defense. Tomorrow we'll meet in the locker room at 3:00," at this coach cast a glance at JD, "We'll pass out uniforms, dress out without pads, and meet right here on the field for a short practice to run through plays, and special teams. Any questions?" When no one had any coach Mac shouted his often repeated question, "Who are we?" At this the team shouted as one "Wildcats!!!!" Then he dismissed them.

CHAPTER 3

Friday night John was on the field early with the backs, receivers and two centers for pregame warmups. He was throwing passes to the receivers as backup quarterback and he still had to do some punting to warm up his leg. After about 20 minutes the rest of the team came on the field to run plays for about 15 minutes, then coach Mac had them return to the locker room to wait for the time to run on the field before the start of the game. He had Coach Archer watch outside the door, as he always wanted his team on the field for the national anthem.

The team sat nervously in the visiting locker room at Western High. The stands had seemed full during pregame warmups. Even though it was a nonleague away game, it seemed as if the whole town had again made the annual 60 mile trip to watch Fort Sage's first game of the year against the Tigers.

In the small visiting office coach Roberts said, "It's about time to go coach, you going to give 'em a big speech?"

"No, no I'm not. Most of these kids haven't played one varsity down yet. I don't want a repeat of last year where we got them so fired up they fumbled every third play," said Mac as he got up to address his team.

"Alright men, listen up," began coach Mac to the

already quiet group of kids. "We know that this is the first game for most of you and we know you're a little nervous. That's good. You play better when you're a little nervous. Tonight I want you to think about fundamentals, fundamentals, fundamentals – every down! Hold on to the ball. Hold your blocks until you hear the whistle. No penalties! Make sure tackles. If you execute tonight just like you have in practice, you'll be fine. Now, let's get out there and get after these guys!" At this, the team all shouted as one and bolted out the door to the field. Mac and his assistants followed. His stomach had butterflies, as it did before every game, even after all these years.

Fort Sage had won the coin toss and had chosen to receive. JD was back to receive the kick with Skipper. 'At least coach has got a few brains,' he thought to himself as he waited for the opposing kicker to approach the ball. He looked over at Skipper who gave him a thumbs up sign, then he took in the whole glorious scene of the first football game of the season, the sweet smell of damp grass, the faint scent of cigarette smoke, the visiting and home stands where everyone was standing up for the kickoff, the cheerleaders rolling their arms in circles, the clean white pants and red jerseys and helmets of the Western team, and his own team's uniforms of royal blue and yellow gold. He heard the referee's whistle, then saw the opening kickoff falling end over end, coming down right where he stood on the five yard line.

He took the ball and broke right following Skip up the side of the field. He dodged one red jersey at the 15 yard line and broke back to his left. He could see in front of him a mass of players in gold jerseys smashing into the red Western defenders. Skipper cut down one incoming tackler at the 18 yard line and John broke back to the right off his block. He saw a gap up the sideline and broke for it with a burst of speed. At the 25 yard line he was hit by a tackler from the side and twisted his body in a circle, breaking free! The visiting crowd cheered as he continued up the sideline at full speed. At the 38 he straight armed another Western player but was knocked out of bounds by a second tackler that hit him square on the shoulder pad, making a loud 'pop'. The crowd roared its approval.

As JD came off the field he felt the hand claps on his shoulder pads and heard Coach Roberts say, "Good job, Douglas." But his eyes were on coach Mac giving Bobby the first play before of the game. 'That should be me,' he thought to himself. He took off his helmet and sat down on the bench to wait until he had to go in on defense.

On the field Bobby faced the offensive huddle and called the 34 blast coach had wanted. On the line he checked the I formation to make sure it was correct, then barked out the cadence, "Ready, Set! Hut, Hut!" He took the ball, spun to his right, and handed off to Silva over right tackle. The solid back bulled into the line for 4 yards and the crowd roared. The same play to the left gained 3 yards on second down, setting up a third and 3. Coach Mac, who was talking to coach Archer on the headset, sent Skip in with "44 cross".

Bobby brought the team to the line, looked over the defense and called his signals. He took the snap from center, turned to his left and faked a handoff to the three back, then whirled to his right and placed the ball in Pete's hands as he headed toward right tackle. Pete

hit the line and seemed stopped as the Western left defensive tackle hit him. He spun and chopped his feet,
knocking the defensive tackler backwards for 4 yards
before he was hit by the two linebackers. As they unpiled, the referee signaled first down!

The Fort Sage crowd roared! The next two running
plays only gained 5 yards, forcing Mac to call a pass.
He sent Skip in with a play called "pro set, slant right."
Bobby barked the signals, took the snap from center
and dropped back for his first pass of the season. He
looked left, saw that receiver was covered, looked at
Skip slanting in from the right and tried to thread the
ball in between two Western defenders. Skip jumped as
high as he could, but he was hit just as the ball reached
his outstretched hands. The ball bounced in the air
and the Western free safety picked it off racing down
the right sideline. Bobby was the only Fort Sage player with any chance at tackling him, but he just wasn't
fast enough and Western player raced into the endzone
with the first score.

After that, the dejected Fort Sage offense couldn't
get untracked and John punted 4 times in the first half.
Western scored again in the second quarter on a long,
10 play drive that had the Fort Sage players hanging
their heads by the end of it. It seemed that every time
one of the Western players took a handoff they were
able to get at least 4 yards and sometimes more, forcing JD, Skip and Bobby to make many of the tackles in
the secondary. There were only 2 passes thrown during
the entire drive and both of those were on the side of
the field away from JD. Now, with only 1 minute left
in the half and up 14-0, Western had the ball on Fort
Sage's 45 yard line, driving again. John looked over

the Western offensive formation as the opposing QB barked signals.

The Tiger quarterback took the snap and dropped back to pass. John began to drop into his defensive zone, but saw a back swing out of the backfield to the left and offensive linemen pulling out and setting up in front of him. John saw the ball floating toward the Western halfback as he raced forward to break up the screen pass. He dodged one of the blockers and leaped in the air right in front of the Tiger back and snatched the ball away with his right hand. As he came down the Western back grabbed his jersey trying to pull him down. John rolled to the right in the direction of the weight then planted his foot and surged forward. The Western player's hand slipped loose and JD stumbled forward, regained his balance and raced down the side-line. He could see the Western quarterback angling in on him from the left. At the last instant John cut left into the Western quarterback's path, throwing him off stride. Then he continued straight into the end zone for Fort Sage's first touchdown of the season!

The half ended with Western ahead 14-7. As they headed for the locker room JD's teammates congrat-ulated him and he saw Wendy in the stands cheering with the crowd, chanting "Douglas, Douglas!" 'Maybe that'll wake coach up,' he thought.

As the second half wound down the Wildcat offense could only produce four first downs. Western was key-ing on Pete's runs and Bobby wasn't throwing the ball well. The Fort Sage defense stiffened and shut down the Western attack by using the adjustments that Mac and his coaches made at halftime.

Late in the game John picked up a fumble caused

by a jarring tackle by Josh and weaved his way 35 yards into Western territory to the 15 yard line. Unfortunately the offense couldn't punch the ball in the endzone. On fourth and 5 at the Western 10 coach Mac called his last time out. He talked with Coach Roberts on the sideline and coach Archer on the headset.

"Mac, we've only got 5 minutes left in the game! We might not get the ball back. The field goal doesn't help us. Let's go for the first down," said Keith. Coach Archer was giving the same advice on the phones.

"No, I don't think so," said coach Mac. "Field goal team get in there." The Fort Sage fans booed to show their disapproval as the field goal team trotted on the field. As second team quarterback, John was the holder on field goals. He broke the huddle, and barked the signals as he kneeled down on the 17 yard line, ready to set the ball. He had heard the coach's discussion, and the fan's disapproval and briefly thought about taking the snap and running for the first down. Josh spiraled the ball straight back when JD blinked his hands. He caught it, and with one smooth motion spun the laces out of the way of the kicker and set the ball on the black tee. He felt Hector's foot kick the ball and turned to watch it go straight through the uprights. Now it was only Western 14, Fort Sage 10!

Unfortunately, after the kickoff, the Tigers were able to grind out 3 first downs, and with Fort Sage out of timeouts, the time ran out. After the clock ticked off the final seconds of their 14-10 loss the Fort Sage players sadly filed off the field. In the locker room coach Mac called his young team together. He knew he had to say something to boost their morale. A loss like this could ruin the entire season.

"Alright men, we lost that one. But don't let it get you down. It wasn't a league game, and we played excellent ball on defense in the second half. We'll work on offense next week and get after Carlyle. You are a good team, remember that. I don't want anyone to lose hope. Of course we want to win every game, but the most important reason we play nonleague games is to get ready for league, and we will be! We're good and we're going to get better, so keep your heads up!" After his short talk, Mac and his assistants walked the locker room giving encouragement to the players, with Coach Roberts making a point to compliment John on his defensive play. Still, it was a long, quiet ride home.

CHAPTER 4

Keith Roberts and George Archer were in coach Mac's office early Monday morning before school, sipping coffee and eating donuts. They wanted to talk to the coach about offense and they knew Mac always wanted things 'his way'. Coach Mac walked in at 7:00 AM sharp.

"Hi Keith, George, what are you doing here so early? Have more news from the Branding Iron Club?" he kidded.

Keith spoke first, "Well, people in town aren't real happy about the loss but we wanted to talk to you about maybe starting Douglas at quarterback this week against Carlyle."

Mac was silent so Keith went on, "He's faster, throws better and is a stronger runner." George nodded his assent.

Mac considered for a few moments then he said, "Guys, I know Douglas is the better athlete. I know we need him at quarterback, but the kid has got to learn he needs all of his teammates to succeed. I don't think his attitude has changed much at all and I don't want him at quarterback acting like he does. It'll ruin the whole team! We'll have people griping that he comes in late, mouths off and then still starts at QB."

"But coach, we..."

"Look, you're going to have to go along with what I want on this guys. I know its bothering you, but that's how it's going to be. Now, how do you think we should attack Carlyle's defense?"

Coach Roberts and Coach Archer looked at each other and shrugged their shoulders.

"We think their secondary is weak, but they've a giant defensive line. They average 245 pounds across their defensive front," said George.

"Umph," grunted Mac.

"We think we'll have to throw a lot more than last week, because we don't think our line can grind this game out on the ground," said Keith.

Mac sighed. 'That's one reason we need Douglas at quarterback this week,' he thought. Then he said, "I think you're right. We'll work on that today and Tuesday. Did Coach Smith and the other freshman coaches get us a scouting report and film on their offense?"

"Yep, got it right here."

"Good, we'll review defense on Wednesday. That is the best part of our team so far. Are you guys going to come to the booster club meeting tonight or let me hang by myself?" The two coaches laughed as they rose to leave, "Naw, we'll be there," said George.

"See you at practice."

Practice that week went just as planned. The team concentrated heavily on their passing game, short slants and outs, as well as swinging Pedro out of the backfield for short dump passes. John was irritated to no end because time after time he would throw better passes, crisp, tight spirals, while operating at the second string quarterback, but still he remained second string. His thoughts of Wendy made him even angrier. Wendy, the way he looked at it, was being stubborn; she wouldn't talk to him all week!

At the end of practice on Thursday, Mac called the team together. "Ok men, everyone take a knee." When they had settled down he continued, "Now, we've got another away game this week. Carlyle has a big defensive line, so Josh, you, Scott and the rest of you offensive linemen have got your hands full, but we feel you're up to it. We are going to try to pass more to loosen them up a bit to take the pressure off. Defensively, we are very confident that we can shut them down. We want to go up there and really put it to 'em early!" Before he let them go, Mac looked at his two assistants and asked if they had anything to add.

"Just this," said Coach Roberts, "it's a long ride up north to Carlyle, so you guys get some rest tonight."

After the 2 hour ride to the Carlyle Kings' field Mac had them dress out and warm up. As always, he had returned them to the locker room for a few minutes to await the time to hit the field right before the national anthem. He always wanted his teams on the field for the national anthem, unlike some coaches that kept them in the locker room until the last minute. The coaches went over last minute offensive and defensive situations before Mac began his usual pregame pep talk. He again wanted to keep it short. The team rested as he spoke.

"Alright, last week most of you got your baptism under fire, played in your first varsity game. Now you're ready. Again, let's stick to the fundamentals. You offensive lineman, hold those blocks as long as you can. Keep your feet wide. On defense we want sure, hard tackles, wrap those arms! You know our game plan. If we execute we should be fine. We can beat this team!" Out of the corner of his eye he saw Coach Archer's signal. "Now men, what are we?"

"Wildcats!" shouted the players.

"That's right, now let's get out there and get after these guys and show them what they're dealing with!" The team jumped up as one, each player's adrenalin pumping hard and ran on the field. Fort Sage again was wearing their yellow gold tops with royal blue numbers and shoulder stripes and yellow gold pants, while Carlyle was dressed out in their home bright green jerseys, with white pants. As John took the field for the kickoff he looked over the stands, the Fort Sage crowd was much smaller this week after last week's loss. He was able to find his mom and little sister in the crowd and Wendy sitting with the small student rooter section.

The opening kickoff had gone to Skipper, and with a good block by John he was able to return it to the 28 yard line. Bobby brought the offense out for the first play, a "pro set, slant pass right" to Skipper. Bobby approached the line and looked over the massive Carlyle defensive line. He barked his signals, "ready, set, hut, hut," took the snap and dropped back into the pocket. The pressure from the defense was surprisingly strong, but since the slant was a quick pass, he was able to throw right before he was hit from the left side by an onrushing Kings defensive lineman. The pass didn't have much zip on it, but it was strong enough to make it to Skip slanting in from the right side. He caught it at the 33 and turned upfield. The Carlyle cornerback hit him at the 35 and knocked him off balance. Skip fell forward to the 37 yard line for a gain of 9 yards!

The Fort Sage team and fans cheered loudly. On second and one coach Mac sent Silva into the line on a played called "split backs, 32 quick." Even though he was hit almost immediately, Pete was able to gain 2 yards in the hole between the guard and tackle. First down Fort Sage!

After a 5 yard gain on a quick out pass to Skip, Bobby was sacked for a loss of 6 yards while trying to pass on second down bringing up a third and 11 play. Expecting a middle distance pass, Carlyle was going to blitz. Fortunately, coach Mac had guessed this and had called the swing pass to Pete coming out of the backfield. Just as Bobby was hit by the onrushing defenders he dumped the ball off in a wobbly pass to Pete in the right flat. He caught the ball in full stride and ran at full speed toward the one linebacker that hadn't blitzed and had come out to cover the pass.

As the Kings defender came in with his shoulders lowered to make the tackle Pete squared his own shoulders and smashed into the defensive man's chest, knocking him flat on his back. Pete then cut to the right sideline and turned upfield. Skip tried to block the Carlyle cornerback, but the defender ran around his block and lunged at Pete, grabbing him around the waist. Pete twisted and surged powerfully ahead dragging the Carlyle defensive back. He could see the Carlyle safety angling over to help on the tackle. Just as he began to lose his balance and go down the tackler at his waist began to lose his grip and slip off. As Pedro broke free he fell forward, stumbling as he ran, with his left hand pushing on the ground to keep him up, his right hand firmly gripping the ball. He came upright. The Carlyle safety smashed into his back and because he wasn't completely balanced he was driven, with lunging steps, into the grass, after gaining a total of 25 yards! As he bounced up from the tackle, his facemask filled with sod, he could hear the fans cheering loudly.

The ball was now on the Carlyle 36 yard line and Mac called a deep flag pattern for Skip. Bobby brought the team out of the huddle and called the signals. He took the snap and dropped back into the pocket, but the Carlyle defensive linemen overpowered the offensive line and he was forced to run to his left. He tried to get back to the line of scrimmage, but the Carlyle defensive end sacked him for a 3 yard loss and the Carlyle fans erupted in cheers.

A second down short pass try to the Fort Sage tight end was knocked down by a Kings linebacker, and a third down slant pass to the Wildcat's other wide receiver was dropped, bringing up a 4th and 13 at the Carlyle 39 yard line. Coach Mac decided to punt, which didn't make the Fort Sage fans very happy, and John went in the game. He took the long snap from Josh and aimed his punt at the 5 yard line on the right side to pin Carlyle's offense deep in their own territory. The ball spiraled out of bounds, crossing the sideline at the 2 yard line, even better than he had hoped. As the Fort Sage defense huddled over the ball, John's teammates were congratulating him. "Great kick JD!" "Way to go Douglas!" The Kings' quarterback was not a good passer, but they did have a large offensive line, using 3 of their massive defensive linemen both ways. Pinned deep in their territory they wanted to punch the ball out of there on the ground. Their first two plays gained 6 yards, bringing up a third and 4.

John watched as the Carlyle quarterback called signals. He was lined up on the strong side at his monster back position. The Carlyle quarterback took the snap and dropped back to pass, this caused the Fort Sage defensive backs and linebackers to drop back into their passing zones. But no! As he drifted into the pocket he handed off to his fullback on a draw. The Fort Sage defenders were caught off guard and the fullback gained 5 yards and a first down before John and Pete tackled him.

The next set of downs weren't as successful and Carlyle was faced with a 4th down and 6 at their own 17 yard line. John dropped back with Skipper to receive the punt. The kick came down high right between both of them on the 50 yard line. John moved over and called for it. When the ball hit his hands he bobbled it for an instant, then got control and headed straight up the middle of the field behind Skip. Carlyle's big linemen were slow covering the punt and John could see this had left a large gap on the left side, if he could get by the onrushing Carlyle end. He cut slightly to the right making the Kings' player head that way, setting him up for a block by Skip. Then he planted his right foot and cut sharply back to his left.

When the Carlyle defender planted his feet to cut back with him, Skip plowed into him knocking him off balance. It was all the edge John needed. He blew past the Carlyle end and raced up the left side of the field. He picked up 2 good blocks by his teammates as he sailed down the sideline. At the Carlyle 20 yard line John saw a knot of green jerseys angling over to cut him off, so he broke his run back against the grain to the right. He ripped through 3 arm tackles and at the 8 yard line he was knocked off balance by a hard hit from the right side, square on his right hip.

The Carlyle defender had hit him hard, but he hadn't wrapped his arms around John when he hit him. The force of the hit propelled him forward to his left, and John twisted as he fell to regain his balance. As he stumbled toward the goal line 3 Carlyle players grabbed at his legs, but too late! He fell into the end-zone for a Wildcat touchdown!

The Fort Sage fans were cheering loudly as the team lined up for the extra point attempt. As the ball was snapped one of the large Carlyle linemen plowed through the line and stuck a hand in the air. Hector's kick was straight, but it hit that big hand and as it sailed wide to the left the Fort Sage fans groaned. Still, the team was up 6-0 at the end of the first quarter and everyone was optimistic.

The second quarter saw Carlyle and Fort Sage trade punts with neither team mounting an offensive threat. As the players filed into the visiting locker room with the lead they were full of fight. In fact, the coaches had a hard time settling them down so they could rest for 15 minutes.

Shortly after Fort Sage kicked off to start the second half it was apparent what the Carlyle coach wanted to do – use his size advantage at the line to run the ball down Fort Sage's throat. Carlyle had the ball 9 minutes of the 12 minute third quarter as they drove from their own 16 yard line to Fort Sage's 10 yard line, by running the ball EVERY play! As the Fort Sage defense huddled there at their own 10 they were all tired. John could see the defense was in trouble and that Carlyle had the momentum.

It had been a bruising drive, with the Carlyle backs getting 3 to 4 yards on each carry. Once, Fort Sage had stopped them at the 48 yard line on a fourth and 4 play, but a defensive face mask penalty had given Carlyle the first down. Coach Mac had argued, but was told by the referee to be quiet or get another 15 yards! The Carlyle quarterback brought up his team to the 10 yard line and began to call signals. The Fort Sage defense was up tight, expecting another run. The ball was snapped and the quarterback turned as if to hand off on another off tackle run to the right. It was a fake, but a very good fake, and the play action pass had caught all of the Fort Sage defenders off guard. As John and the other defensive backs moved up to make the tackle, the Carlyle quarterback pulled the ball out of the halfback's belly, took two steps back and lofted a soft pass toward the right corner of the end zone. The Carlyle end was wide open and he softly cradled the ball for the touchdown. The try for the extra point was good and Fort Sage was behind now 7-6.

The rest of the third quarter was used up as Fort Sage ran three plays and punted. The fourth quarter began with the teams trading punts and now, after another stalled drive, Fort Sage was forced to punt with only four minutes left in the quarter. The offense had twice produced two first downs in a row, but erratic passes and a very questionable offensive holding call had stalled the drives. Now Carlyle had a chance to run out the clock, with the ball on their own 29 yard line and only three and a half minutes left in the game. The defense broke their huddle with the knowledge that they had to have the ball back, NOW. A first down sweep to the right was stuffed for a 2 yard loss by Paul. On second down the Carlyle fullback gained 4 yards off tackle bringing up a third and 8. The Carlyle coach, not wanting to risk an interception, tried to run a counter play to the left, but Scott and Pete both held their positions at left tackle and linebacker and stopped it for no gain. This brought up 4th and 8, and Carlyle had to punt, but there was only one and a half minutes left to play with the clock running, as coach Mac was saving his last time out.

The Wildcat fans were all hoping John could get a good runback on the punt, maybe even a score. The King's punter avoided that by smartly punting the ball out of bounds on the Fort Sage 48 yard line. The Fort Sage players were optimistic, they only needed about 30 yards to get inside Hector's kicking range.

The first two pass plays fell incomplete, with Bobby under heavy defensive pressure. On third down he dropped back and threw a floater in Skipper's direction. Skip adjusted his pass route and caught the ball in between two Carlyle defenders on the Carlyle 30 yard line! The clock stopped as the referees moved the chains for the first down. When it started again there were only 45 seconds left.

Coach Mac decided to use the swing pass to Silva that had been successful earlier. Bobby brought the team out of the huddle with 33 seconds showing on the running clock. He called signals and dropped back to pass, dumping the ball off to Pedro on the right side again. Pete was able to break one tackle and head up field, but because he had caught the ball behind the line of scrimmage, when he was swarmed by green jersey's he had only gained 3 yards. With 19 seconds left on the clock, coach Mac had to call his last time out.

The ball was on the Carlyle 27 yard line, making a field goal 44 yards long. Hector had never kicked one beyond 35 yards. Mac and his assistants discussed their options during the time out. Keith argued for one more pass up the deep middle on the chance it might catch Carlyle napping and Fort Sage might score. Mac disagreed and sent Bobby in to call a quick out to Skip. Carlyle expected just this sort of call and they had both Fort Sage wide receivers covered, forcing Bobby to throw the ball out of bounds. It was 4th down now and the only thing to do was try for the field goal. Fort Sage broke the huddle and lined up.

The green jerseyed defense was fired up to try to block the kick, their players jumping and yelling. JD took the snap and smoothly set the ball down. Hector swung his foot into the ball as hard as he could, and the football sailed high toward the goalpost. It seemed as if everyone in the stands and on the field turned to watch that football tumble end over end toward the goal post. But, Hector simply couldn't kick that far and the ball fell 5 yards short, causing the home crowd to erupt. The green and white Carlyle players danced and yelled as the Fort Sage players hung their heads and slowly filed off the field after shaking hands. A 7-6 loss was a bitter pill to swallow.

In the locker room coach Mac told his team they had nothing to be ashamed of, they had played very well. That the defense had again played great. That next week was their first home game and they were going to win it. But it was a glum ride home and as he rode the bus back to Fort Sage he kept thinking about what the townspeople would say, and he knew what it was. If Douglas had been at quarterback, there's no way they would have lost that game. He knew they would say that, because he knew it was true.

CHAPTER 5

John received a note during first period asking him to see the junior class adviser after school. He didn't want to, but was on his way to Mrs. Johnson's room when he ran into Wendy, also walking across campus.

"Hi JD!" she said, "You played real well Friday."

"Thanks, too bad I wasn't playing quarterback," he replied petulantly.

"Ah, JD, I wish you'd quit being so sour. Things can't always go your way. Where are you going anyway?" said Wendy.

"I'm on my way to see Mrs. Johnson. I received a note in class today to see her after school, I don't know what she wants."

"Really, I'm going to see her also," she said knowingly. She hadn't mentioned the plan to JD yet, but she was sure he'd be interested.

Mrs. Johnson looked up as they walked in. "Oh, I'm glad you came in kids. I wanted to talk to you about the annual Octoberfest the high school puts on."

John glanced at Wendy who beamed as she returned his look. Mrs. Johnson continued, "I've talked with Wendy briefly, John, and I could really use both your help in organizing the production. We really only have two months to prepare, the 'fest' is scheduled for the last week in October. What do you think?"

"It'll be great!" bubbled Wendy, "When do we start? Wouldn't that be great John? We can't wait to get going! Right JD?"

John was taken aback. He hadn't known anything about this! He was very irritated. Didn't these people know he was busy?

"Well, what about the class officers?" he asked.

"They're all going to be busy with fund raising for the Winter Ball, and Junior-Senior prom and besides, this is a school wide project. I need someone I can count on, someone I think can get things done." She paused, seeing the scowl on John's face. She had never been one to beat around the bush. "Will you help John?" she asked directly.

"Of course he will," blurted Wendy. "We'll do it together! I knew you'd help JD. That's why I volunteered us! Great, huh!"

"No!" he said angrily. He didn't like being put on the spot. And he didn't want to be a part of anything, he wanted to be on his own. "I've got other things to do. Right now I'm going to practice. You should asked me first! I'm out of here!" John said as he turned and stomped out of the room.

Wendy was stung, and embarrassed. "I'll help Mrs. Johnson, don't worry, I'll get others to help to. I'm sorry John was so rude. I'll check in with you next week, OK?" Tears began to well in her eyes.

"It's OK Wendy," Mrs. Johnson said gently. She could see the tears in her eyes. "Thanks for your help."

"I don't know what's bothering him," Wendy said, "Goodbye." Then she raced out of the room to catch John.

"JD!! Wait!" she called as she ran down the sidewalk

after him. When she caught up with him she couldn't hold her anger in. "What is your problem!? You were very rude to Mrs. Johnson, and another thing, I thought this would be fun! I think you owe everyone an apology!"

"Well, I don't! Look, I don't want to do that. I've got other things to do."

"Oh yeah, like what?"

John thought for a few seconds. "Well, it doesn't matter, I just don't want to do it."

"Well why not? You're so stuck on yourself! I'm sick of your whining!"

John didn't want to talk about the Octoberfest. He didn't want to argue with Wendy, and he couldn't understand why she was being so unreasonable. He tried to change the subject. "Hey Wendy, this Friday's our first home game."

Wendy was still mad. "Yeah, so what!"

"Well, there's a dance in the gym afterwards and I thought you might go with me."

"Right now I don't think I want to go anywhere with a spoiled kid like you!"

"What? You mean - no?" John asked almost incredulously.

Wendy thought for only a moment. "Yes, JD, it does mean no. You've changed since last year," she said simply.

This hit John like a slap in the face. He was sure Wendy would never say no, after all, he was the best player on the football team. His pride was hurt, and he struck back. "Oh yeah, well that's fine with me! There are other girls. See you around." John turned and walked toward the gym. Wendy stared after him through her teary eyes.

As he put his pads on for practice, John thought about what he had done, and began to regret it. 'It'll be alright, I'll make up with her,' he thought to himself. I'll go talk to her on the way to the practice field. After dressing out, John walked out onto the gym floor in his pads and practice jersey looking for Wendy at volleyball practice. He found her across the gym warming up by bumping the ball with another player. He walked across the floor toward her. She didn't even look at him, but he kept going.

"Wendy, can we talk?" he asked when he was close enough for her to hear.

"I'm practicing, can't you see. You better get to your practice before coach Mac gives you some more laps!"

"Oh, don't worry about that," said John, coolly.

"I don't care one way or the other because we don't have anything to talk about," snapped Wendy. Embarrassed, John made his way out of the gym.

The cloudy, grey sky seemed to match the team's mood at practice that Monday. Coach Mac knew that if his team didn't win this week they might not win again. Confidence played a big part in high school athletic performance, and right now his team was lacking that. It seemed that no matter how good he told them they were, or how much he cheered, they simply did not have any fire. It was so bad he finally sent the team in 15 minutes early then he met with his assistants in his office to talk about the problem.

"Guys, we've got to get this team going. Right now they don't have any confidence, and darn it, they're a good team. We should be 2-0 instead of 0-2. I think we better be very positive with them all week. Avoid criticism at all costs, let's tell 'em how good they're doing," said Mac.

"I think that's a good idea," said George, "but we've got to get the offense going. The only times we've scored have been because of Douglas."

"Why don't you start him this week at quarterback?" prodded Keith.

"No. Absolutely not. He still thinks he's the greatest thing on earth. The kids won't follow him."

"He's the best we've got and we need him," said George, "What's wrong with thinking you're the best if you are, anyway? You just said the team needs confidence."

Mac thought for a moment. "Nothing, really. Except, no matter how good you are, you always need your teammates, and Douglas hasn't learned that yet. He's arrogant...big head."

"I think you're being a little too hard on him. Besides, is it fair to the rest of the team to not play him? The other kids want to win to you know. You're hurting the other kids. That is not fair," said Keith very directly.

"You've both made your point," said Mac, "but. . ."

"Don't say it," interrupted George, "we already know, you want it done your way. Coach, if I had one complaint, which I don't; that would be it. But, you're the head coach, so I'll go along with your decision."

"I guess I will to," said Keith, "after all, your head's on the block. Going to the booster club meeting tonight?"

"I'm afraid I have to," said Mac, "although I think we all know what we'll hear after we show the films." Mac stayed to lock up the locker room after the two coaches left. Maybe they were right, he thought. This was the first time they had ever really disagreed with him. Maybe he was hurting the team just to try to get Douglas to shape up. But no, if the best athlete was allowed to slide, be late, talk back, then soon the whole team would be doing it. What he needed was for Douglas to LEAD, not let everyone know how good he was. But, you couldn't stand up at a booster meeting and say things like that. They wanted wins! He felt his stomach start to tighten again.

Friday morning John sat in his 3rd period US History class, daydreaming, which was unusual because he loved history; it was his favorite class. He was in a bad mood, in fact he had spent the entire week in a hopelessly bad mood. Wendy acted like he wasn't even alive, and wouldn't talk to him. Here he was sitting right next to her in class in his bright royal blue jersey, which the players wore to school the day of every home game, and she wouldn't even look at him. Practice had gone OK all week, no one had "got on his case", but coach still would not let him start at quarterback, and because John knew he was the best quarterback, this made him even more angry.

He was thinking about how he had popped off to the town newspaper reporter yesterday and wondering if he had gone too far by telling him straight out that he should be starting at quarterback, and the team would have won the first two games if he had, and that he wasn't sure the coaches knew what they were doing. He had a sinking feeling that it might cause him trouble.

His thoughts were interrupted by Mr. Smith, his teacher, who was also the freshman football coach. "Mr. Douglas, could you answer the question?" His teammate Scott reached across the aisle and nudged him out of his daydream. John didn't even know what the question was.

"Um, well, um, could you repeat it?"

"No, I'm not going to repeat it! Maybe you should get your act together!"

John was embarrassed, and the kids laughing at him didn't make him feel any better.

"I want to see you after class Mr. Douglas."

After the bell rang, John remained to listen to Mr. Smith tell him that he was disappointed in him and that his last test grade was a C not his usual A or B. That his approach to school work seemed to be changing, and that he might call his mother. When Mr. Smith finished, John left to go to lunch. "What a bazoo," he told Scott, who had waited for him. "Doesn't he know I have a game tonight? He can't treat me like that!"

Scott simply said, "I like Mr. Smith a lot. He is the best teacher I've had."

"Pffft," was all John would say to that as he walked off.

Later, after school, John arrived two hours before game time with Skipper and Pedro to dress out and have his ankles taped by Coach Roberts just like all the rest of the backs and receivers. At about the same time, coach Mac, sitting in his office, opened the day's paper to read the write up about the game that night. John was sitting on a table in the locker room when Coach Archer came in.

In an angry tone he said, "Douglas, coach wants to see you in his office, NOW!"

"Man," said Skip, "What did you do?"

John suddenly had that sick feeling in his stomach. Coach Mac must have just seen the paper. He got off the table without answering and walked into the office thinking that maybe he did go a little far with that reporter.

When he entered coach Mac was standing by his desk with his arms crossed. "Read the paper yet Douglas?" he asked in a very unhappy tone.

"Well, no I haven't," said John.

"Then let me read you the headline, that about covers it," said coach Mac icily, "Here it is - Wildcat Player Questions Coaches." He showed the paper to John and watched while he read the article. "Well, what have you got to say?"

John didn't know what to say. He had told the reporter what he thought was true, but he could see coach Mac was probably angrier than he could ever remember. He thought about apologizing, then his immature cockiness got the best of him. "Well, Coach you know it's true."

Mac was livid. He had seen cocky athletes before, but this kid took the cake. "Douglas, you just don't get it do you? You are only one player! ONE! This is a TEAM!" he literally roared. "Until you decide to be a part of the TEAM and work with the other players, you're on the bench."

"But, But.." John stammered. "I, you can't, I..."

"This discussion is over," said Mac forcefully.

John started to say something, but Coach Archer took him by the arm and led him out to the locker room.

"Just go dress out Douglas. If you know what's good for you, don't bother coach anymore today."

John went in the locker room and sat down on the bench in front of his locker. Skip and Pete went over to ask him what happened. They could tell he was upset and angry. But John wouldn't talk to them, he simply shook his head back and forth. He did not enjoy being treated like that. He couldn't believe coach would not play him, the best player on the team. 'First Wendy dumps on me, now coach,' he thought to himself.

"Well, I don't need this," he said loudly, slammed his locker shut and stomped out of the room. He stuck his head in Mac's office on his way out and shouted, "I'm out!"

Skip and Pete had watched him go with worried expressions, then they had heard him shout.

Scott, usually reserved and quiet, called over to Pete "What the heck was that about?"

"What the? Skip, I think we better go talk to coach."

"I think you're right, come on!"

CHAPTER 6

S kip and Pete knocked on coach Mac's door, then entered when he said come in. Mac and his two assistants were standing in the office looking at the newspaper and shaking their heads.

"What can we do for you boys?" asked coach Mac.

Skip and Pete looked at each other, then Pete swallowed hard and spoke. "Um, well, coach, uh JD seemed pretty upset when he came out of the office, and well, he wouldn't tell us what was wrong, and, well, he just took off. We were wondering if you could tell us what happened."

Mac looked at the two juniors, wondering what to do. Usually he didn't discuss one of his players with any of the others. But, he sincerely wanted to help young Douglas and these two were his best friends. He picked up the paper and handed the sports page to Pete and Skip. "This happened," was all he said.

As Skip and Pete read the paper their eyes almost popped out of their heads. They couldn't believe John had said those things to a reporter! They looked up at the coaches, not knowing what to do. They stood silently, shocked.

Finally, after an uncomfortable silence, coach Mac said, "Just before you came in here he opened the door and yelled 'I'm out'. You said he 'took off'?"

"Yes," the boys answered.

"Where did he go?"

Skip and Pete exchanged glances, then shrugged their shoulders. "Why was he so mad?" asked Skipper.

"Boys, I've never told other players what I've said to someone privately in my office, but in this one case I will. I told Douglas he was on the bench until he learned to be a part of the team," said Mac. "Anything else?" Coach Mac waited.

As he waited his thoughts were racing. He wanted the boys to ask if they could go find Douglas, but he didn't want to tell them to. It was much more than winning or losing. In fact, it had nothing to do with winning or losing! He had grown up with Douglas's mother; he didn't want to ruin her son, yet somehow he was worried he was doing just that, what with his dad gone and the way things had been going. When the two boys didn't say anything he said, "Well, there's almost two hours before game time. I thought you two might want to leave the gym for some reason."

This seemed to jar Skip out of his stupor. He smiled his big, white smile, looked at Pete and said, "Let's go."

As they walked out the door, he turned to coach Mac and said, "We'll find him coach." Then they were gone.

After the door shut, Coach Roberts looked at first George, then Mac and said, "Do you think he'll come back?"

Coach Archer just shrugged his shoulders. Coach Mac, suddenly feeling very tired, answered, "To tell you the truth, I don't think we'll see him play football again." He sighed, shook his head and sat down. It was things like this that made his hair turn grey.

For 30 minutes Skip and Pete drove around town,

looking for JD. They had gone to his house, but his little sister hadn't seen him. They went to the park, down Main Street; they couldn't find him anywhere. At last, Skipper decided they had to go tell his mom. It was their last choice; they had to get back to the gym. They drove over to the hospital where she worked as a secretary, parked the car and walked in the lobby.

They found Mrs. Douglas working behind the front desk. She looked up as they approached the counter.

"Well hello boys, what are you doing here? Don't you have a game in an hour?" she asked. Then she noticed they were worried. She felt her gut tighten. "What's wrong?"

Skip spoke, telling Mrs. Douglas about the newspaper story, then about their conversation with coach Mac. John's mother sat down, her head in her hands.

"Mrs. Douglas, we've got to get back. He won't answer any text messages or cell calls. Do you think you can find JD and talk to him?"

"Yes, yes, I've got to," she stammered, her voice breaking. "Thank you boys for coming to tell me. Now you better get going. Try not to worry."

After the boys pulled away, Mrs. Douglas explained the situation to her supervisor and she left to go find her son. As she drove home on the verge of tears, she felt herself floundering. She simply did not know what to do. Her son was in trouble, just this week two of his teachers had called to say his grades had dropped from A's to C's. Now he pulled this stunt with the newspaper. What was wrong with him?

"Oh James," she said aloud, "I wish you were here." Where had her son gone? What was wrong with him? She had a nagging feeling that his father's failure to return from the Iraq war, and his listing as a probable KIA, had started this change in behavior. She remembered that he had never cried about it, and had refused to even discuss it, so she had let the subject go, thinking that he needed time to heal. And now this latest incident. She was very worried that she was losing her son. Where could he have gone? She thought of his favorite place. In every house, no matter where they had been stationed, it was the room where her husband had kept his trophies. In their house in Fort Sage it was the little office her husband had added to her bedroom. She decided she would try to find him there.

When Mrs. Douglas walked in the door, her daughter Mary looked up at her red, puffy eyes and knew she was upset. "What's wrong mommy? There were two boys here looking for John, is he OK?"

Mrs. Douglas pulled her daughter to her, "Yes, yes, he's OK, he's just a little upset. Have you seen him?"

"No, I've just been playing computer games since I got home."

"Alright, you go ahead." Hoping she was right, she said, "I think I know where he is. I'm going to go talk to him, now, can you stay here Mary?"

When her daughter nodded yes, Mrs. Douglas gave her a kiss on the head, hugged her, and walked down the hall. She entered her bedroom quietly, then crossed over to the small office and nervously peeked in the room. She let out a sigh of relief when she saw John sitting on the floor, his arms around his knees pulled up to his chest, staring at his dad's sports trophies. She went in and sat next to him. For a long time neither of them said anything. She wanted so much to hug him and comfort him, to fix his problems. Finally, she said,

"John, you look so miserable. Skipper and Pete came to see me at work. They told me what happened. Do you want to talk about it?"

John looked over at her. "No, No I don't. I'm not going to play football anymore. I don't need football, or coach Mac, or Wendy, or anyone!" Mrs. Douglas considered his statement. Her son was so troubled and here she sat feeling as if she didn't have a clue as to how to help. As they both looked at the trophies without seeing them Mrs. Douglas knew she couldn't let her son go on like this. What she decided to say she knew could be devastating to him, but the way she looked at things, she must. She had tried to reason this out for the last month. What she wanted to do most was sympathize with him, but she knew she couldn't.

"John," she said softly, "I think you need to take a hard look at the way you've been acting." His head jerked up in protest, but she raised a hand to stop him and continued in a soft voice. "Please, let me finish. Your teachers have called to say your grades have dropped. You've become rude and sullen. You haven't been to Sunday mass in months. Now, this thing with the newspaper reporter, well, I can't believe you did that to your team."

JD looked at her and started to speak. Again she stopped him. "Let me finish, please." When he stopped, she began again in her soft, yet strong voice. "John, I love you dearly. My heart aches to see you so troubled. The last thing I want to do is hurt you, but what I'm about to say may. I want you to listen, carefully."

She stopped herself, hesitating, then forced herself to continue. "John, we've never talked about your dad since he was lost. He loved you, more than you'll ever realize. You and your sister were his hope and joy. He was so very proud of you both. And you, well, you were his only son, his ... sometimes I thought he loved you more than me." Mrs. Douglas stopped again. Her throat had a large lump in it and she felt tears forming in her eyes. She didn't want to go on, she could see the pain already showing on her son's face. "John, I'm disappointed in you. And I know this, your father would never, never have approved of the way you've been acting, and he never, ever, would have let you walk out on the team after what has happened today." 'There,' she thought, as she rested her head in her hands, 'I've said it.' When she looked at her son she saw tears begin to well in his eyes.

John sat on the floor in his dad's office, thoughts of his father swirling through his head. His dad had been his best friend, his pal. He thought about the times he had played catch with his dad as a young boy or played one on one in the driveway, going camping and fishing with him, listening to his dad tell his old sports stories. He remembered the hours his dad had spent showing him technique and giving him pointers, the times they had sat watching sports on TV, and the times his dad had proudly showed him off at the helicopter flight line at the base. How he had adored his father! All of his life his dad had been with him, played with him, taken the family places, and then he was gone, and he never came back. As vivid as if it had happened yesterday, John remembered the last thing his dad had said before leaving,

"Take care of things JD, help your mother, and get in shape! I'll be back before your first varsity game!"

Then they had shaken hands. As this last thought

raced through his mind John's right hand involuntarily reached out, as if to take his father's. John had never even considered the possibility of his dad being shot down, he had always come back before. John blankly glanced down at his empty hand and he began to cry, for the first time, about his father. The tears spilled down his cheeks as he looked at his mother and tried to speak through his tight throat. His voice quavered and jerked. His shoulders heaved.

"Mom," he said, "It just isn't fair." He sobbed, his breath labored. "I miss him so much. Why didn't he come back? Is he really dead? We don't even know for sure! It seems like every second I think about where he is! He could be trapped in some terrorist prison... I have this ache in my heart and I can't fix it...it never goes away...Why didn't he come back? Why?"

As Mrs. Douglas looked at her crying son her heart broke and she couldn't control her own tears. She reached out, put her arm around John's shoulder and pulled him close. Through her tears she tried to answer, her own voice halting and quavering. "I don't know why his gunship went down. The Army said he took a direct hit from a modified Stinger missile. In wars, I guess, these things happen. He's still listed, officially, as missing in action-presumed dead, but. . .but we both know. . .he's gone. I feel it. I know it. I would know if he were still alive on this Earth. It's hard... so many others made it out alive.... I can tell you the last thing he wanted to do was to leave his family, it was his worst fear... He agonized over his orders to ship out. He even considered resigning his commission. But it was your father's duty to go."

She stopped, unable to go on, and they cried

together for a short while. Finally, Mrs. Douglas gathered herself and continued. "John, as you get older you will discover life is not a beer commercial. Sometimes, it gives you a plate full of unhappiness – for no reason. But, do you remember how your dad talked about how the importance of teamwork on a football team was the same as the need for teamwork in a helicopter gunship. He was the team leader, the pilot, and he had to go, he was part of the team. Your father was a man of courage, and honor. He was a wonderful man and God knows I miss him every day of my life, just as you must. Sometimes I become so angry! I know you must feel so cheated, and angry. But your father's spirit is here with us; he'll be with us always in our hearts, we can carry him with us every day. We've got to go on living. He would want us to, and he would want us to live in a way that would make him proud of us. That's what I try to do, and that's all you have to do. You've nothing else to prove. I know it's a hard thing to accept, especially since we weren't able to bury him... to put it behind us, but we can't shut off the rest of the world."

Mrs. Douglas paused, reflecting, then said, "You need your teammates just as much as they need you, just like your father needed his crew on the helicopter, and they needed him." She rubbed her son's shoulders as his sobs slackened and then came to a stop. Then she added, quietly, softly, "And your little sister and I need you. We both love you so much." She handed him a tissue to blow his nose. John sat for a few moments next to his mother thinking.

She was right, he knew. His dad would never have approved of his actions. He had asked him to help his mother. Was that what he was doing? What about his sister, was he helping her? John suddenly felt selfish and very ashamed. He had been such an idiot! He had dishonored his father. A thought came to him. "Mom, what time is it?"

"It's almost six-fifteen, why?"

"Well, do you think if I get back to the gym and get dressed out before the team hits the field things will be OK?"

"I don't know," she answered honestly. "I think it's worth a try."

"I've got to get going. The game starts at 7:00." John said as he rose to his feet. As he made his way to the door he felt like a load of bricks had been taken off his shoulders. He turned at the door, "Mom, I'm sorry I've been so much trouble. I love you," he said simply and was gone.

CHAPTER 7

As John briskly walked and jogged the few blocks back to the gym he thought of what his mother had said and he resolved to change. He was going to try to start acting like the young man his dad had tried to raise. He made up his mind to honor his father's memory, not tarnish it. He had a lot to make up to a lot of people and he was going to start today. At 6:25 PM John literally burst into the coach's office. Coach Roberts and Coach Archer were already on the field with the kickers and backs for their early warmup. He could hear coach Mac getting the linemen ready to go out for the team warmup. 'Thank goodness he's still here,' John thought. He waited.

When Mac entered the office again to get his clip board he saw John sitting by his desk, his head hanging. He felt both anger and relief at the same time. He started to speak, but John spoke first.

"Coach, um, well, could I talk to you."

"Make it quick, I've got to get on the field."

John was nervous, his arrogance out of him. He stammered, "Well, um, coach, I wanted to say I'm sorry." Then he sighed, shook his head and took a deep breath.

Mac looked him in the eye, his hands on his hips, "Just sorry, that's it? That's supposed to make everything OK?"

"No, no, I, well, I know what I did was wrong, and I know that I've been acting like a jerk. I wanted to tell you if I want to be a part of the team." The pressure he felt was almost too much. "I really want to be a part of this team. I realized today how important that is."

Mac considered this for a moment. It seemed as if something had knocked all the wind out of Douglas's sails. He knew it took a lot of guts for a kid to do what Douglas was doing. He was fully aware of what Douglas's family was facing. He was silent for a full 10 seconds considering what to do. After all, it was why he had sent Wilson and Silva to find him. Finally he said, "Well, I think we can arrange that. Provided you can get dressed and on the field before kickoff!"

John just about leaped off the chair, then Mac spoke again.

"Slow down son, slow down now. Remember what I said earlier, about showing me you want to be part of the team. Saying it is not enough. Until then, you're on the bench. Can you handle that?"

Even though he wanted to play, John was relieved that coach had let him back on the team. "Sure," he answered.

"Alright, get dressed out and get out there."

"OK coach, and thanks," said John. Then as Mac turned to leave he said "Um, coach?"

Mac turned, "Yes?"

"Well, I thought that I ought to apologize to the team."

Mac paused and thought for a moment. "That'll be hard to do. You sure you want to do that?"

"Yes," John said firmly, his jaw set.

"OK, you'll have your say. But not tonight, not right

before kickoff. You can address the team Monday before practice, now get dressed."

"Thanks, coach," John said then he beat Mac out the door to get into the locker room.

As Mac walked the rest of the team out for pregame warmups he wondered about Douglas. What had happened to him? It was one thing for Douglas to apologize to him, but it'd take some fortitude to face the whole team. Whatever had happened, Mac felt like he was dealing with a new person, and it made him feel good.

Thirty minutes later the team entered the locker room hot and steamy from pregame warmups. Mac asked Coach Archer in a low voice to check with the referees on how much time they had left. He surely didn't want to miss the national anthem at the first home game of the season, nor get a penalty for delay of game. He turned to his silent team. He began in his easy, controlled voice. "Alright men, tonight we play our first home game! Our stands are going to be packed. You people get your minds on football. WE ARE A TEAM! TEAM! We have to play together to succeed. Nash, like I told you earlier, you're in on defense as the monster back in place of Douglas. We've been over and over the Twin Buttes offense all week and we know they're fast, so don't get beat deep on pass plays."

He saw coach Archer's signal from the door so he knew he only had a couple of minutes to finish up. "You men are a good football team! Right now we should be sitting here with a 2-0 record. We all know that this is our last nonleague game, and the coaches firmly believe this team can take the league title! We want to go out there tonight and show the fans and Twin Buttes that we can play with class! We want to execute our plays with precision. We want to win this game and give River Bend and the rest of the league something to think about all next week! Now," and he looked each player in the eyes one by one, "WE CAN DO IT. WE CAN WIN THIS GAME! THIS TEAM HAS THE ABILITY."

The intensity level of the team began to rise, he could see it. "Are you with me?" he asked. The Fort Sage players roared their assent. Then Mac growled loudly, "Let's GO!!" The players began to file out of the locker room excitedly. "GO!" shouted Mac. "GO!!" His talk had lit a fire under them, and he was relieved, although not much of a speech was necessary because this was their first home game of the season. The kids were naturally "up", even though they had been lackluster in practice all week.

When the last one had burst through the door coach Roberts looked over at him and said, "Good to see Douglas back!" Mac nodded his agreement as they left to make their way out to the field. As he jogged out toward the home sidelines Mac was optimistic about their chances that night, even though he wasn't going to play Douglas. As always, the butterflies began to act up in his stomach.

John ran on to the field in the back of the pack of Fort Sage players. Full of jumbled, conflicting emotions, he viewed with near awe the spectacle of the first Fort Sage home football game of the season. Adjacent to the high school campus, and taking up two full city blocks the "stadium" was the result of the high school's football state championship years and the continued serious local interest in football.

The field ran east and west and was probably the

best football field in the league, better than the fields in much larger towns they played against. The rigid aluminum stands easily held 2500 people on each side and supported a large press box high above the home stands. The bright, halogen field lights sat high on steel poles behind the stands, not in front by the field, as some schools had them. The rich green, immaculately cut Bermuda grass was highlighted by white painted yard lines, red end zone markers, and bright yellow-gold goal posts. It emanated that certain sweet, wet grass smell mixed with cigarette smoke JD always noticed before games. The packed stands of the home crowd, already buzzing with the news of that evening's sports pages, had stood and let out one long roar as the Fort Sage players had burst on the field through the paper sign reading 'Beat the Cougars' held up by the cheerleaders.

The Fort Sage team was resplendent in their royal blue jerseys, with yellow gold letters, and yellow gold pants with two royal blue stripes down the side. They seemed to John as if they were hallowed knights approaching battle as they jogged down the sidelines to the bench.

John wore his number 23 with pride; it had been his father's number in college. He remembered how he had wanted so badly to get to this moment in time, his first varsity home game! He had daydreamed about his dad up in the stands watching him hit the field, leading the team, but that was not to be. His dad was gone, and he would not play tonight. How he wanted to play! How he wished his dad was here to watch! Nothing had gone as he had hoped! Nothing. As he stood on the sidelines, cradling his golden helmet, listening to the national anthem, tears slowly rolled down his cheeks and he resolved to do whatever it took to show coach Mac he wanted to be a part of the team, whatever it took to get back in the starting lineup.

After the national anthem the game captains, Bobby the senior quarterback, and Paul the defensive end, met at midfield for the coin toss. When the referees signaled Fort Sage had won the toss the home crowd again roared their approval. They were hungry for a victory!! Coach Mac had already decided to receive if they won the toss and so he called for the kickoff receiving team to meet with Coach Roberts. Habitually, JD took a step toward the field, then remembered his situation and melted back into the jumble of players along the sidelines. He looked for his mother; he hadn't had time to tell her how things had gone with coach! He saw her high in the stands along the western end of the bleachers at the 30 yard line sitting with his sister. When she saw him turn his head she waved to him.

Embarrassed, he turned back to the field but somehow she had made him feel better. He didn't bother to look for Wendy, he didn't think she would even acknowledge his existence. She was someone else he had a lot to make up to. The head referee blew his whistle and JD gave his full attention to the game.

The Twin Buttes players looked sharp in their visiting white jerseys and green pants, highlighted with gold stripes and numbers and green helmets. As their kicker approached the ball to begin the game, J.D. wondered why teams that wore white always looked so big! The kick sailed high and long, down to the 3 yard line where Skipper cradled it and began his return right up the 'middle wedge' that coach Roberts had called for. At the fifteen, a Twin Buttes tackler got an arm on his right hip which slowed him down and caused him to veer to the left. Still running at the 20 he stutter-stepped to cause another Twin Buttes tackler to miss, but was swarmed under at the 25 by four white jerseyed tacklers.

Bobby, who had been waiting on the sidelines, ran in with the first play, a simple dive between the right guard and tackle. Fort Sage broke the huddle with a large clap of their hands and ran up to the line of scrimmage, setting up with a tight end to the right side, flanker left, split end to the left. Bobby surveyed his team, checked on his split backs, then barked the signals. At the second hut he took the football and spun to his right, planting it right in Pete's stomach.

Pete grasped the ball, and lowered his shoulders as he plowed into the line of scrimmage. The pile of blue and white players seemed to move in slow motion forward to the 30 yard line before it stopped and the slowly crumpled to the grass. He had gained 5 yards! The home crowd yelled and cheered! Mac sent in the guard with next play, I formation, dive left. Again Pedro took the hand off, this time to the left, and bulled for 4 yards before he was hit hard below the waist by a Twin Buttes linebacker and brought down. On third and one Mac called for the same play he had used to start the game. Pete again gained 5 yards! It was now first and 10 on the Fort Sage 31. Mac, following his conservative philosophy, which was "if it's working, run it until they stop it", called for the same play again. Out of the split back formation Pete gained 3 yards on the dive to the right. On second and 7 Pete powered off right tackle, through the "four hole" between Scott and the tight end for 4 yards! On third and 3, working out of the I forma-tion he gained 4 yards to the left, through the "three hole" between guard and tackle. Fort Sage had a first down on the Fort Sage 42 yard line!!

Mac then dove Pete straight up the middle on first and second down, once to the left and once to the right. Pete had gained a total of 6 yards and Twin Buttes had started to stiffen in between the tackles. Thinking for those few seconds between the time the runner and tacklers unpiled and the referees marked the ball for the third down play at the 48 yard line, Mac considered a counter out of the split back formation, then decided to go to a pitch outside off of a fake to Pete up the mid-dle. Ross, the halfback, hadn't even touched the ball yet, and Mac was guessing that the entire Twin Buttes defense would swarm toward the fake to Silva up the middle.

Bobby called the play and broke the huddle. He barked his signals, "Blue... Ready... Set... Hut, Hut, Hut!!!", took the football and seemed to plant it right in Pete's stomach for the same dive to the right they had been running. As the Twin Buttes defensive line and linebackers swarmed toward Pete, Bobby pulled the ball out and pitched to Ross breaking toward the left end. The Cougar defense was caught totally off guard and sucked way in toward the middle, just as Mac had hoped. The Wildcat left guard had pulled to the left and was out in front of Ross as he rounded the left end. Skip, the wide out to that side had run the defensive corner off deep and Ross had a clear field in front off him. The Fort Sage guard aimed a block at the recovering outside linebacker and was able to nick his shoulder, knock-ing him off balance, and cause him to miss the tackle.

Ross turned upfield, into the secondary and it seemed he might score. But, the Twin Buttes team was fast, and their secondary recovered quickly and flew toward the ball. Ross, not as fast or quick as JD, was unable to out-run them and was chased down from behind, but not before he had gained a whopping 25 yards! As the fans stood and cheered, the referees marked the ball for a first down play at the Cougar 27 yard line.

Not wishing to ruin a good thing, Mac sent a guard in with a play calling for Pete to plunge into the line off left tackle. He literally bulled his way forward 4 yards then popped up from under the pile to run back to the huddle. It was his way of showing the Twin Buttes de-fense that he wasn't tired at all, even though he had carried the ball 9 of the last 10 plays. On second down Mac called a straight dive to Ross in the two hole on the right side.

Although a little faster than Pete, Ross wasn't near-ly as strong, and he was only able to gain 2 yards, which brought up a third down and 4 at the Twin Buttes 21 yard line. Mac, figuring he was in 4 down territory, didn't consider a pass. He briefly thought about an-other pitch to the outside, but figured that was exactly what the defense would expect. He ran a guard into the huddle with the counter he had almost called earlier.

The play, called "33 counter left", had Bobby fake a dive on the right side to Ross, then after pivoting around until his back was to the line of scrimmage handing off to Pete who would hit the left side of the line in the 3 hole. The Twin Buttes defense, reacting to the first action of the offense, went for the fake to Ross. The two Cougar linebackers stepped up to tackle Ross and by the time they realized he did not have the ball, Pete was at the line of scrimmage and easily broke through their arm tackles. He ripped into the secondary, eating up yards with his seemingly slow, yet powerful stride. The two Twin Buttes safeties came up to make the tackle, lowering their shoulders. Pete cut to the right and aimed directly at one of them, lowered his own shoulders and smashed into him, throwing up his free forearm and using his legs for leverage just at the instant of impact.

The defensive safety bounced straight back, flat on the ground as Pete plowed over him. The other safety managed to grab onto his shoulder pads, but Pete pulled him five yards before finally stumbling and falling down - over the goal line!! A 21 yard run for the game's first touchdown! The home stands were roaring as Hector's point after kick, with Bobby holding for JD, made the score Wildcats 7, Cougars 0. What a drive! It had almost been picture perfect, 11 plays, all of them on the ground.

Against the faster Twin Buttes team it was exactly what Fort Sage needed to do, control the ball and run the clock. Coach Mac glanced up at the clock as coach Roberts sent the kickoff team on the field. His team had used up nine and a half minutes of the first quarter on that drive. Things were looking very good so far!

In spite of his ache to be in the game, JD had grabbed Pete's hand and shook it as he came off the field after scoring. He was happy for his friend, and he was glad the team was ahead. He walked up and down the sideline congratulating the offensive team. Some of them readily accepted his congratulations, others were still skeptical. JD was unconcerned; he was determined to be different, starting tonight.

The Twin Buttes kickoff returner was quick, very quick. He returned the kickoff back to the Twin Buttes 44 yard line before he was tackled by Skip, the kick-off team safety man. Though down on the score board, Twin Buttes was not lacking self-confidence. They had a 2-0 record, good team speed, and a quarterback that could throw. They quickly went to work offensively to even the score. Their quarterback took the first down snap and dropped straight back to throw. He looked to the right, but the right end running a deep post pattern was covered well by Skipper. He looked back to the left and saw his flanker ahead of Ross on an out and up pattern. Though pressured by Paul his throw was straight on the money, 30 yards downfield! The Twin Buttes receiver caught the ball in full stride streaking up the left sideline. He would have scored if Skip hadn't been able to run him down and make the tackle on the Fort Sage 20 yard line. As the referees moved the chains the Twin Buttes crowd cheered lustily.

Twin Buttes tried a dive up the middle on the left side, but Scott, the right defensive tackle, made the tackle for only a one yard gain. On second down, with the ball set on the left hashmark, Twin Buttes ran a sweep around the right end. Paul, the defensive end, played off the block of the pulling guard, turned the play to the inside and was able to help Josh make the tackle after a gain of 3 yards. The Cougars now faced a third and 6 on the Fort Sage 16 yard line. Trying to use his speed, the Twin Buttes coach had his offense come out in a pro set formation with a wide receiver left and another wide-out and flanker right. When the ball was snapped, the 3 receivers ran patterns into the endzone and one back swung out of the backfield as the quarterback dropped into the pocket. He didn't have much time as Paul again was pressuring him from the right side. The quarterback dumped the ball off to the back that had swung out of the backfield just as he was hit by the onrushing Paul. The speedy Cougar back caught the ball and eluded Josh's attempt to tackle him at the line of scrimmage. He darted to the left and right wiggling between tacklers down to the 8 yard line for a first down.

Twin Buttes tried a pitch around left end on first down that gained only 2 yards, setting up a second and goal at the Fort Sage 6 yard line as the clock ticked off the last seconds of the first quarter. As the teams jogged down to the other end of the field, Mac heard Douglas yelling encouragement to the defense. 'We'll need more than that', he thought to himself, 'a fumble or interception would be real helpful.'

The Twin Buttes coach, sensing that his success was going to come in the air and not on the ground, called another pass play on second down, the first play of the second quarter. It was a crossing pattern between the right wide out and the left tight end. The Twin Buttes quarterback took the snap and rolled to his left, sprinted around the Wildcat defensive end that was caught rushing too tight, and looked in the end zone for his wide receiver crossing from the right. As the Fort Sage linebacker and recovering defensive end closed in on him he twisted his shoulders and fired a bullet to his wide receiver that had gained a step on the Fort Sage monster back, Ross. The home fans let out a large groan as the receiver caught the pass for the touchdown. The point after kick was good and in less than 3 minutes Twin Buttes had evened the score 7-7.

The remainder of the second quarter mirrored the

first. Fort Sage took the kickoff and Mac kept the ball on the ground, grinding out 2 straight first downs. They faced a third down and 7 at their own 43 yard line when Mac, again crossing up the defense, called for a draw play to Pete instead of a pass. Pete busted up the middle for 10 yards and what seemed to be a first down, however, Fort Sage was flagged for holding and penalized 10 big yards. Facing a third and 16 Mac had reluctantly tried to pass and Bobby's attempt to reach Skipper on a deep out pattern had sailed high out of bounds. With 4 minutes remaining in the half, Fort Sage, with JD on the bench, was forced to use their back up punter. He punted the ball down to the Twin Buttes 35 yard line.

Twin Buttes took the ball and came out firing passes at the Wildcat defense. While Skip had the speed to cover the Twin Buttes receivers, Ross did not. In order to avoid another long completion, he was giving a large cushion, and as a result Twin Buttes was able to complete passes in front of him. Three passes gained two first downs and moved the ball to the Fort Sage 40 yard line. With two minutes remaining and the clock running, the Twin Buttes quarterback barked his signals, took the snap and dropped back to pass. He looked at his wide receiver breaking his pattern out to the right deep in Fort Sage territory, but he was well covered by Skipper. He glanced quickly to his left, saw his left wide receiver curling in behind the Fort Sage corner, Bobby, and in front of Ross. He fired his pass on target.

The completion put the ball at the Fort Sage 25 yard line! With only a minute and a half remaining and the clock ready to start again after the referees moved the chains, the Cougar coach called for a timeout. It was actually a lucky move for the Fort Sage defense. With so many players playing both offense and defense they were starting to get winded and several were bent over in the huddle with their hands on their knees.

During the time out, Coach Roberts told the linebackers to watch for the draw play, then suggested to Bobby a pass could easily come toward him or Ross, as they had been picking on that side of the defense. As he left he told Paul, his returning all league defensive end, that they needed a hard pass rush. The Twin Buttes quarterback took his instructions back to the huddle and called his play, a "pick" pass route between the left wide receiver and left flanker back. They were going to try to rub off either the Fort Sage corner, Bobby, or the monster back, Ross. He brought his team to the line and barked his signals over the noise coming from the home fans stomping their feet and letting out a long, drawn out "aaawwwww". At the snap he dropped quickly back and looked to his left, waiting for the wide out or flanker to clear.

In their defensive coverage, Bobby had the wide receiver and Ross the flanker back. The two offensive receivers crossed their patterns but neither Bobby nor Ross stumbled or fell. Bobby maintained tight coverage on his man, but Ross began to lose a step as the flanker turned upfield. The Twin Buttes quarterback saw this, as well as the royal blue jersey bearing down on him. He cocked his arm to throw and as his arm came forward Scott plowed into him stopping his arm about halfway. The pass floated off his fingers like a wounded duck and Bobby broke off his coverage to make a diving interception on the 15 yard line. The home stands roared their approval; the defense had held!

Deep in his own territory, and not wanting to risk and interception, Mac called for 3 straight running plays that gained a first down and burned off the last Twin Buttes time outs. With the ball still only on his own 26 yard line he had his offense run the ball 3 more times to run out the clock and end the half.

As he led his team to the locker room, Mac knew they were going to half to do something about the Twin Buttes passing attack.

In the steamy locker room at half time the two assistant coaches, wanting to win the first home game badly, approached Mac about inserting Douglas into the defensive secondary to help with pass coverage. Mac was almost offended by the request.

"Guys, Geez! Have you lost it? You know I can't do that, not after what's happened," said Mac angrily.

"We need him in there, Mac," added Coach Archer.

Mac frowned. He was not happy and the two assistants knew he was not happy. He cleared his throat, and looked away, thinking. "You guys want to win this game badly, don't you?" he asked, then added before they could answer, "So do I. But this involves more than winning and losing. We're talking about self-respect, what Douglas feels for himself, what his teammates feel for him, and for us; and what we feel for ourselves. If he plays tonight after all that's happened, we might as well kiss this team goodbye. That kid is a great athlete, you know it, I know it, God, the whole town knows it. But he's got to EARN his way back into the starting lineup. I think, for whatever reason, he's turned the corner, made a start. But he'll have to show me and his teammates he means what he says. We just can't put him in there."

Coach Archer and Roberts were silent. They knew Mac was right; in fact, they both felt a little foolish.

"Alright, offensively we're fine. Defensively, Douglas is not an option. What can we do to stop that passing attack?" asked Mac.

After about 5 minutes of discussion, the coaches agreed to try to pressure the Twin Buttes quarterback with some blitzes and defensive line stunts. They also decided to drop out of the "monster" alignment and go to a straight 5-2-4 defensive set up to try and relieve some of the pressure on Ross in his man to man coverage. After reviewing these changes with the team, the coaches led them back on to the field for the second half kickoff.

Fort Sage had to kick off to start the half and the Twin Buttes returner got the ball up to the 35 yard line. The Twin Buttes quarterback came out firing passes left and right. In three straight completions he had advanced the ball down to the Fort Sage 30 yard line which had the roughly 300 hundred visiting fans fired up and making noise.

On first down from the Fort Sage 30 yard line, with the Fort Sage defense reeling, he barked his signals, took the snap and took a quick three step drop. The play his coach had called had four receivers in the pattern, two running deep outs, one crossing over the middle, and a back looping out of the backfield.

He floated a touch pass over the outstretched fingers of Josh, the Fort Sage left linebacker, into the hands of his tight end, who caught the ball and headed up field for a 24 yard gain before he was tackled on the 6 yard line by 4 Fort Sage defenders. With a first and goal on the Fort Sage six yard line, the Twin Buttes coach tried a run off tackle to the left which was stuffed for no gain by Josh filling the hole. On second down Twin Buttes again went to the pass with four receivers in the pattern. But, as a passing team gets closer to the end zone the room for pass patterns is reduced and in some ways the shorter yardage favors the defense, making it easier to cover receivers. Without any receivers open and under pressure by Paul again, the Twin Buttes quarterback threw the ball away out of the end zone. With the ball on the left hashmark, the Cougars tried a screen to the defense's left on third down.

Scott, playing a great game, saw the back pull out to the right as he rushed on the pass. He pushed hard off of the offensive tackle that had picked him up, turned and ran to the outside toward the back. The Cougar quarterback, under pressure due to the nature of the execution of the screen pass whereby the offensive linemen on the right had blocked for two counts, and then released their blocks allowing the linemen to rush, was forced to throw a hurried pass over Scott's hands.

His pass sailed high, over his halfback's head, incomplete. The home crowd yelled their relief and continued to roar a loud "aaaawwwww" as the Twin Buttes quarterback brought his team out of the huddle to go for the touchdown on fourth down. It was another pass attempt, this time a roll to the left. With his receivers again covered, the Twin Buttes quarterback tucked the ball under his arm and headed for the corner of the end zone. Bobby, the corner, reacting to the run, came up fast to make the tackle. He hit the Twin Buttes quarterback hard with his left shoulder, causing a loud "pop" heard all over the field. The home stands cheered lustily as the runner was knocked out of bounds on the one yard line! The defense had held again!

Bobby's tackle had been hard and as the Wildcat offense huddled in the end zone the Twin Buttes quarterback walked off the field holding his right shoulder with his left hand, grimacing in pain. It appeared he would be out for the remainder of the game.

The rest of the third quarter was used up by Fort Sage on another long drive on the ground down to the Twin Buttes 35 yard line. Mac faced a second and seven with the ball on the right hashmark as the fourth quarter began. He wanted to run as much off the clock as he could and still score. Two more runs produced a first and ten at the Twin Buttes' 26 yard line. Mac went back to the I formation and called Pete's number straight up the gut for 3 yards. On second down, from the 23 yard line, he called for a fake to Pete up the middle out of the "I" and a pitch to Ross around the left end.

Ross only gained 2 yards and now Fort Sage faced a third and five on the Twin Buttes 20 yard line with the ball on the left hashmark. The clock was running and showed 8 minutes left in the quarter as Mac sent in his guard with a counter play to Ross out of the "I" formation. It only gained 3 yards to the disappointment of the crowd. Now Fort Sage faced a 4th and 2 on Cougar 18 yard line. Mac debated with himself while the referees marked the ball, then called for the field goal team. It was not a popular decision with the fans who were yelling "GO, GO, GO!"

The home crowd became silent as Hector stomped his foot to show Bobby where to place the ball. Just before the ball was snapped Twin Buttes called time out, trying to get Hector nervous. After one minute the teams lined up again, and Hector prepared to kick the ball on an angle from the left hash mark. The defensive line surged forward as the snap came back sure from the center and Bobby placed the ball. Hector swung his leg, his foot meeting the ball with a "thump". His kick was true as it left his foot, then, as if perpetual bad luck was sitting on Fort Sage's sideline, a long arm stretched out from the Twin Buttes defense. One of their linemen had penetrated deep into the backfield and threw his arm up as the kick sailed off Hector's foot. The football just glanced off the defensive lineman's hand and wobbled off to the right side. It sailed long enough, but wide to the right. No good!! The home crowd groaned and became angry, most of them had wanted Mac to go for the first down anyway. Mac hung his head for a moment, then realizing he had to get his defense "up", he raised it, clapped his hands, saying over and over "That's OK, we'll get it back!"

Twin Buttes took over on their own 20 yard line after the missed kick - with their second string quarterback. They were able to gain a first down on the demoralized Wildcat defense at the 32 yard line after 2 passes and a short run. Their second string quarterback was a little shakey, and after getting planted hard on his back by Paul, Fort Sage's defensive end, on first down, he was even more so. He brought his team up to the line for the second down play, still thinking about the last hit he had taken as he called his signals. The center slammed the ball up in his hands at the second "Hut!" but the nervous Twin Buttes quarterback couldn't grab it cleanly. The football squirted out of his hands under his legs. With the Fort Sage defense screaming "Fumble!" he turned to jump on the ball, kicking it with his left foot. The ball bounced crazily to the side where Scott, the Fort Sage tackle, pounced on it! The referees jumped into the pile of players emphatically signaling first down Fort Sage on the Twin Buttes 25 yard line! The home crowd went wild!

With a little more than 5 minutes left, Mac knew what he wanted to do. Score and run the clock out! He returned to the "I" formation that he had success with earlier, running Pete up the middle for 5 yards. Two more runs gained a first down at the Twin Buttes 14. A short side sweep to the right gained 4 yards down to the ten yard line. The four running plays had eaten up almost 2 minutes and the clock now only showed 3 minutes left! Mac called a counter to Ross out of the "I" formation on second down that didn't go anywhere. He now faced 3rd and 6 from the ten yard line with the clock running.

Trying to cross up the Twin Buttes defense and figuring they would be tight up the middle, Mac called for a double split end formation, with split backs. The play called for a counter sweep left to Pete behind the right guard pulling out left. It was a risky call down close to the goal line, requiring many offensive players to go several directions. Bobby called his signals "Blue, Ready, Set... Hut, Hut, Hut!" He took the snap, pivoted and faked a handoff to Ross who was supposed to fill the hole left by the pulling right guard. He pulled the ball out of Ross's stomach and was hit by a Twin Buttes defensive lineman that had followed the pulling guard and knocked Ross aside! Before his knees touched, Bobby reached out and flipped the ball into Pete's hands. Pete bobbled it, got a handle on it, and accelerated toward the left end zone corner. His lead guard was able to nick the linebacker coming up to make a tackle and all that remained between Pete and the goal line was the defensive corner that had fought off Skip's block. The corner came up and hit Pete low and hard, and was surprisingly able to drag him down short of the goal line at the one!

The clock showed less than two minutes after the referees marked the ball indicating a first down. Mac tried a quarterback sneak on first down that didn't gain an inch. Twin Buttes called another time out to stop the clock at one minute 30 seconds. A second down dive up the middle by Pete was again stopped short of the goal line, bringing up a third and goal at the one-half yard line. Twin Buttes gambled and called their last time out to stop the clock at one minute 15 seconds.

Mac approached the offensive huddle and looked at the excited faces of his players. They're almost too ex-ited, he thought. He didn't want them to make a costly mistake at this point.

As the Cougar coach exhorted his players to stop Fort Sage two more times Mac said to his huddled offense, "Alright, you guys just settle down, settle down. Now, we're through messing around with this team. I want wedge blocking, double tight ends, Silva dives it right behind Scott on the right side! We are going to score! Get it done." Then he walked off the field to watch.

JD and the rest of the Fort Sage players were massed at the edge of the players box on the sideline, watching. Bobby called the signals, took the snap, and slammed the ball into Pete's stomach. He plowed into the line off tackle, shoulders low, as Scott pancaked the Twin Buttes left defensive tackle. The pile fell forward into the endzone, touchdown Fort Sage!!!

The players were so excited, they forgot to line up

for the extra point in time and were penalized 5 yards for delay of game, much to Mac's displeasure. However, Hector converted anyway for a 14-7 lead and only a minute remaining in the game.

After the kickoff, Twin Buttes made it interesting, advancing the ball to their own 48 yard line. But without timeouts, they simply ran out of time. The home fans shouted out the final ten seconds and the Fort Sage Wildcats exulted in their first win of the season!! JD joined the team as they danced on the field, holding their helmets high in the air. He specifically sought out Scott and his two close friends, Skipper and Pete, to congratulate them on winning.

As the two teams lined up to shake hands a few home team parents spilled out on the field to talk to their sons. JD filed down the line of players shaking hands with the other team filled with mixed emotions. It had been great to see the team and his friends win. He ached to have been with them! He somehow felt left out of the whole thing and the thought occurred to him that he now knew what it was to ride the bench for a whole game, to be one of those teammates he had called "losers" early in the season. He told himself he would never make that mistake again.

After the teams shook hands, Mac called his excited group together for some congratulatory words, reminded them that next week was their first league game and that he knew they were ready now, and then he sent them to the showers with a final "Have fun at the dance and stay out of trouble!" Most of the team trotted in to the locker room to get ready for the after game dance, while a few remained behind to talk with their parents. JD was walking slowly off the field when he saw his mom and little sister talking to coach Mac near the fifty yard line. 'Oh boy, what's mom up to?' he thought. He decided to wait for her and moved over near the fence that ran along the edge of the field. He saw Mac shake his mom's hand, pat his sister on the head, and begin to make his way to the locker room. He went to his mom to ask her what was up, but before he could, she spoke.

"John. . ." she stopped, and JD could see she was having trouble talking. She seemed upset and he could see the beginnings of tears in her eyes.

"Mom, what's wrong? What's happened?" he asked urgently, suddenly worried.

"Nothing, nothing, it's just that, well....coach Mac told me what you said to him tonight. I want you to know I'm proud of you."

Relieved, JD didn't know what to say. He was a little embarrassed.

"Ah, well. It was just something I thought I had to do. You were right about everything mom," he said. "Look, I better get going before they turn the lights out." He turned to leave, then his sister called out, "Hey, John, are you going to the dance?"

JD slowly turned and said, "No, not tonight. I guess I'll just come home. See you later." As he walked into the locker room his thoughts turned to Wendy. Would he ever get her back?

At home that night, JD wrestled with his conflicting emotions. He was glad that they had won, but he felt so left out. He was so unsettled he had declined Skip and Pete's offer to go have a burger after the game. As he settled into his bed that night he vowed to stick it out, whatever the outcome. He had promised himself he was going to change, and that was what he intended to do.

CHAPTER 8

S aturday morning found JD up early. He wanted to mow the lawn for his mother before he went downtown. He hadn't done it since football practice started and it had now become a mess. When he finished, he cleaned himself up and headed down to Main Street. Usually he would have just goofed off all day, but he had made up his mind before he dropped off to sleep the night before that he needed to get some type of part time job to help his mother out, and that was his goal today.

The first four businesses he stopped in at didn't need any help and weren't hiring. He was beginning to get a little discouraged when he found himself in front of the local Quick Gas station. He wandered around the garage area for a couple of minutes before the owner, a hard lined, gray haired old man came out.

"What can I do for you, youngster?"

"Well sir, I was wondering if you needed any part time help?" asked JD.

Old man Franklin was a town institution and an avid Fort Sage sports booster. Those that didn't know him thought him a mean son of a gun. He really wasn't, in fact, if you needed help and he had a way to do it, he would. He had run his station for nearly 40 years and had occasionally employed part time help, mainly from the local high school. He liked to help out the athletes whenever he could, but just now he wasn't going to spill all of that out to the young kid standing in front of him. He wanted to feel him out a little first.

"Well now," Mr. Franklin said, "part time help. Humph! I been running this station for nearly 40 years by myself, why would I want to hire some part time help?"

JD did not know Mr. Franklin and he felt like he had irritated the old man. He considered leaving, but decided to give it one more shot.

"I... I was hoping I could get some type of part time job to earn some spending money, maybe save some for college. I just thought you might need some help. I didn't mean to get you mad. If you don't, well, I don't want to bother you." JD turned to leave.

"Now hold on there, kid! I ain't done with you yet! What's your name anyway? What grade are you in?" asked Mr. Franklin.

JD stopped and turned, "My name is John Douglas. I'm a junior over at the high school."

A knowing twinkle appeared in Mr. Franklin's eyes. "John Douglas, John Douglas. Hmmmm. Seems I read something in the paper about a John Douglas last week." At this JD began to blush. "Hey, do you play football?"

"Um, well, yes I do," said an embarrassed JD. He figured the man had read the article in the paper about what he had said about the coaches. 'That's it for me,' he thought to himself.

Old man Franklin grinned to himself. "So you're the hot shot quarterback, huh? Didn't see you in the game last night."

JD was thoroughly nonplussed. He didn't know what to say to the old man. He wanted badly to get away. "I...I...I didn't, well, I wasn't allowed, no, well, I just didn't play."

Mr. Franklin had already heard the whole story from Mac himself when he had come in for gas earlier that morning. In fact, Mac had worked for him as a high school student. The last thing Mac had told him was that he thought young Douglas had "turned the corner." Mr. Franklin had been surprised to see him at his station asking for a job, but now that Douglas was here, he had decided to hire him. He just wanted to have a little fun first.

"Well, why not? Thought you were pretty good? ... Well?"

JD did not answer. He felt horrible, terribly humbled. He just stood silent.

"Oh, alright, don't know why I'm doing this but I guess I could use someone to help around here. You ain't going to pop off to the paper about me are you?"

JD blinked. He couldn't believe what he had heard. His face showed a look kind of like a scared rabbit.

"Hey, I'm asking you a question kid! You want the job?"

"Um, No!, No, I mean yes! Yes, I want the job! And, no, I won't talk to the paper about you!" JD finally responded.

"Good grief, kid, hope you're not always in such a daze! When do you think you can work?"

"Well, I could work for you on weekends. I can't do much after school, what with practice and school. Would that be OK?"

"Humph! I suppose we could work that out. Can

you give me 8 hours every Saturday? 9 to 5? If you can, I won't make you work on Sunday."

"Sure, sure! That'd be great, that way I can go to mass with my family on Sunday," said JD. He stood waiting and a car pulled up to the gas pumps.

"Well!" said old man Franklin. "Well? What do you want?"

"Um, when do you want me to start?" JD asked.

"Kid, is today Saturday? It is, isn't it?"

"Yes, yes it is."

"Well, you said you'd work on Saturdays. Now, get out there and help that customer!" Old man Franklin laughed his deep throated laugh as JD jumped out the door and ran to the car. "Crazy kid doesn't even know what to do!" 'Oh well,' he thought, 'I guess he can figure it out.'

As JD fumbled with the pump he blessed his luck. He couldn't wait to tell his mother. "But geez," he said to himself, "that old man. Hope I can put up with him! Crusty old guy!"

"What's that kid?" he heard Mr. Franklin yell out of the door.

JD jumped in his shoes, "Oh nothing, nothing. Just talking to myself, Sir."

"Sure kid," laughed Mr. Franklin out loud, "Sure!"

At 5:00 PM Mr. Franklin called JD over and paid him cash for that day's work since it was the last Saturday in September, then told him that he would get a check every two weeks from then on.

"There you go kid," he said gruffly, "see you next Saturday."

"Thank you Sir!," said JD excitedly; he had never had a real job before. "Thanks a lot! I'll be here next

Saturday!" John then made his way out and toward Main Street.

"Hey kid!" called Mr. Franklin when JD was at the station's corner, "Hey kid!"

John turned, "Yes Sir?"

"Don't be late!" Mr. Franklin hollered in his most gruff tone. "I heard you're late sometimes!"

"Oh no sir. No, I won't be late," John answered, wondering who had told the old man that.

As he made his way down the street he wondered why Mr. Franklin was laughing.

"Mom! Mom!" John called as he burst in the door. He was bubbling over with excitement. He had never had a real job and he was very proud of himself. "Mom?"

"What is it dear? And where have you been all day!? I tried to call you on your cell," he heard her ask from the back yard. He went out and found his mother and little sister laying in the hammock under the tree.

"Good grief! What happened to your clothes?"

"You smell like gas!" said his sister.

"That's because I got a job today!" beamed JD.

He saw his mother's jaw drop. "A job? Where?"

"Down at the Quick Gas on Main Street. See, I got paid today to!" said John as he proudly showed off his twenty dollar bills.

John's mother had to stifle her urge to giggle at her son. Still so much like a little boy, she thought to herself, then said with a smile, "John, that's great! What made you do that?"

"Well," John put his head down, "I kinda felt like I wasn't much help around here so . . ." Then he held up he held up his money again, "Hey, let's all go eat dinner, my treat!"

"What? Oh don't be silly. You keep your money."

"No really Mom, I want to take us all out to eat."

"Yeah!" yelled his little sister, "I want pizza!"

"Come on Mom," said John, "when was the last time you got to eat out? Let's go."

"Ah, come on Mom, pleeeease," begged his little sister.

"Well, OK! Let's go. But first you go take a shower!" As John bounded back in the house Mrs. Douglas couldn't help but feel very proud of him.

On Monday, JD made sure he got to school early. He wanted to talk to Mrs. Johnson about the Octoberfest which was only two weeks away, and he didn't want anybody to know he was talking to her. She looked surprised to see him waiting at her door when she walked up at 7:45.

"Hello John, what brings you to school so early on a Monday?"

"Well I was wondering if I could talk to you about the Octoberfest."

"Hmmm, really? Come on in," she said as she unlocked the door. When she was settled at her desk, John went on.

"I was wondering if you still needed help," he said.

She considered. She didn't really need help, but the more help she had the better. "Well, yes, we could use some help. But, I thought you said you were too busy to do this."

John turned a little red, "I know I said that, and well, I shouldn't have. I'm not that busy and I've thought about it. I'd like to help you if I could. Maybe I could deliver things, pick stuff up for you, do things like that."

"OK, sure, that would be great. Can you meet with Wendy and the others she has lined up to work on this project Wednesday night?"

John hesitated. That wasn't really how he wanted to do this. "Well, Mrs. Johnson, I was wondering if I might help you out on the side, so that the others wouldn't know about it. I kind of don't want to make a big show of it."

Mrs. Johnson rested her chin on her hand for a moment. She thought she knew what John was getting at, but to be sure she asked, "Is it a certain young lady named Wendy you're not wanting to know about your helping?"

John sighed, "Well," then he paused, " Um, ...yes."

"Alright then, you must have your own reasons. We'll keep this between you and me. Check with me after school and I'll give you a list of little jobs and errands you can do for the Octoberfest committee, uh, anonymously, shall we say?"

John smiled, "Thanks Mrs. Johnson. I'll see you after school." Then he left to make his way to the library. As he turned out the door he bumped into Wendy coming in, knocking her books down in the doorway. They both bent down to pick them up at the same time and smacked foreheads, sending Wendy sitting down on the floor rubbing her head.

"Oh, geez, I'm sorry Wendy, are you alright? Is your head OK?" John asked as he gathered her books.

"I'm OK, I'm OK," said Wendy quickly.

"I, didn't see you coming in, I . . . I . . . I'm . . ." JD didn't know what to say. He felt like a complete idiot. He handed Wendy her books as she got to her feet. Their hands touched, and as if shocked by electricity, separated. JD again felt the pain of her breaking up with him. He wondered what Wendy was feeling. She looked up at him, then giggled slightly.

"We must look pretty comical to Mrs. Johnson," she said.

John laughed slightly, "Yeah, I guess we do. Are you sure you're OK? I, I, .. I didn't mean to bump your head."

"I'm OK. Forget it. I've been hit worse than that on the volleyball court. What are you doing here so early, anyway?"

John glanced knowingly at Mrs. Johnson, "Oh, well, I had to clear up an assignment, that's all. Well, I, uh, I've got to get to the library." JD looked at Wendy; their eyes met, filled with regret. He wanted to ask her to meet him later to talk, but he was afraid she would refuse. She waited for him to ask her to meet later, afraid he wouldn't. "Well, I uh, I need to get going, bye," was all that he could get out, then he left.

Wendy watched him leave, suddenly wishing he hadn't. She had felt the need to talk to him, but she didn't want to tell him that, still feeling angry with him. "What was he doing here? Hmmm. I wonder what he is up to," she said softly to herself.

CHAPTER 9

M ac was in his office early, 6:00 AM sharp, as usual, on Friday morning. The team lifted weights Monday through Thursday from 6:30 to 7:30. Friday was game day so they had the day off. He nursed a cup of coffee and munched on a leftover donut while he sized up this week's game with River Bend. River Bend was going to be tougher than Twin Buttes. It was going to be each team's first league game and River Bend had finished second in the league last year to Central Valley. They were a strong team and he knew they would test his young, but talented team.

Practice that week had been very smooth. His mind went back to JD talking to the team Monday before practice in the locker room. When everyone was together, Mac had quieted down the whispers then said, "John has asked me for permission to talk to you, I gave it. Douglas, you've got the floor."

John had stood up on suddenly knees that looked weak. All eyes were on him. He had swallowed, but the lump in his throat stayed there. He began, "I, I, asked coach to talk to the team because . . . well, I . . . I feel I owe everyone an apology." John had let out a big burst of air, like he had been holding it underwater. No one said a word, everyone had eyed him keenly, especially the seniors. 'They don't believe him,' Mac had thought. Well, he had understood why.

Douglas had doggedly persisted, "I, I know I haven't been fair to all of you. And what I said in the paper was wrong, I shouldn't have done it." He had looked at the three coaches, "We've got good coaches, and you're all good players, and I, ... well, I just wanted to say I'm sorry to all of you, and well. . . I really want to be a part of this team. I realized how important that is." Finished, he had sat down with his head hung low on the verge of tears. The locker room had been silent. No one had made a sound. Mac had never seen anything like it. Mac had turned to his silent team.

"Alright men, Douglas has had his say. He knows what the score is as far as being on this team. It's up to each of you to decide how you feel about him. Just remember," Mac had paused, "remember that we are a TEAM. Each one of us has blown it big time at some point in our lives. I've talked with John," using his first name unusually, then continued, "I believe him."

As he thought more about it he realized that the Douglas kid had guts. He also realized that some on the team would never accept him back again. But, the team's morale was high after their win, and Mac had been more relaxed. Young Douglas had not had one argument with him all week, even though he was still keeping JD on the second team offense and defense. He knew Douglas didn't like it, but Mac could see the kid was determined to grit his teeth and keep silent. Douglas had got himself in this mess after all.

JD had done his best to run the River Bend offense against the Fort Sage defense in practice, sometimes too well, ripping off chunks of yardage against the first team defense. He tried to pump up the second string offense when they ran plays. And sometimes, Mac had to admit, they looked just as good as the first team. Douglas had hustled everywhere he went on the practice field. He wasn't late, in fact, he was early for every practice. He complimented his teammates on good plays. In short, Douglas was trying to become the team leader that Mac had wanted all along. There were still some skeptics on the team, but Mac knew the majority of the players were slowly beginning to believe that what JD had said Monday might be true, and they were starting to accept him. The question was, should he allow Douglas to start this week. Mac had mulled it over and over and was still considering this when his two assistants walked in at 7:15.

"Coach, I don't think we'll ever get here before you," said coach Roberts as the two assistants sat down in chairs.

"Man, Friday came fast this week," said Coach Archer.

"Well, they have a tendency to do that during football season," Mac said. "League starts tonight guys, and it'll just get more hectic from here out."

"Mac, are we going to use Douglas this week?" coach Roberts asked, "seems like everyone in town, including me, wants to know."

Mac looked his assistants in the eye. If he only considered winning and losing, the smart thing to do was start Douglas. But he felt in his gut the need to keep him out one more week. He didn't want the young man to get off too easy for what he said in the paper, and it had only been 7 days since the story had been written. He also had to consider the rest of the team.

Mac had sensed the rest of the team was coming around but he felt they needed more time. He knew many people in town were surprised by the article, but at the same time, he knew many people in town agreed with what Douglas had said. The pressure had eased this last week because of their victory last Friday, but it was always there. Another loss and the wolves would be out with a vengeance.

"Well, what do you two think?" he asked the two assistants.

Coach Roberts spoke first. "Mac, that kid is our best athlete. We need him in there. Without him we are much weaker on defense and with him our offense is more powerful. I'd like to play him."

"Me too," said coach Archer, "besides, you know this is our first league game. We need to get off on the right foot."

"We won without him last week, didn't we?" asked Mac.

"Well, sure. But Twin Buttes wasn't nearly as strong a couple of our league teams will be, especially Central Valley," said George.

"Guys, is this ONLY about winning league games? I think for the good of Douglas and the team, this kid needs to sit out one more game. He's coming around, sure. He had a great week in practice. But we don't want to make this too easy on him."

"Then again," said coach Roberts, "we don't want to knock the wind out of him, just when he's coming around do we? I mean, is it fair to the other 25 kids to not put our best players on the field? Those kids have goals and they want to win also."

Mac paused, thinking hard about what coach

Roberts said. After a long minute he said, "No, no we don't want to ruin him. But, I'll have to ask you guys to go along with me on this again. He doesn't play this week." At this the two assistants groaned. Mac went on, "If Douglas is the same next week, then we'll get him in there."

Disappointed, the two assistants left to get ready for their morning classes, leaving Mac alone at his desk. When they had walked about half way across campus, George spoke.

"Keith, do you think we can win without Douglas?"

"I don't know George. We won last week, but...." he shook his head, "I don't know about old Mac. He sure has to have things his way all of the time."

"Yea," agreed George, "Heck of a guy though."

"Yea, that he is, that he is. Sometimes I just wish..." Keith let his thought go unfinished, but both assistants were thinking the same thing. Coach Mac was not one to take advice from people.

As the bell rang ending his last period English class, JD quickly made his way for his mom's car. He had borrowed it that morning to pick up some decorations for Mrs. Johnson and now he had to deliver them before reporting in to coach Mac, then heading over to the hospital to give the car to his mom. He pulled the car over to the curb closest to the English buildings. As he unlocked the trunk, he looked around to make sure Wendy wasn't around, then gathered his arms full of plastic flowers and paper and hurriedly made his way to her door. Mrs. Johnson had seen him coming and held the door open for him.

"Thanks, John, just put them over there in the corner next to the stuff you brought in on Wednesday."

JD made two more trips before he was through. As he dropped the last batch he spoke, "That's the last of them, Mrs. Johnson, need anything else today?"

"No, no that's it for today. There'll be some lumber to pick up next week, and some booths. But I don't think you can get those with your car."

"Well, let me work on it," said JD, thinking of Mr. Franklin's pickup. "Maybe I can arrange something."

"Really, John, I can put in a work order with the office."

"No, No, I'll get them!" then, looking out the window, he saw Wendy coming. "Uh, oh, I better get. I'll talk to you Monday about the wood and booths, OK?"

"Oh, alright. Thanks for your help. I'll see you then," smiled Mrs. Johnson.

John slipped out the door, and because Mrs. Johnson's class was on the end of the building he was able to make his way around the corner before Wendy started coming down the breezeway from the other end.

Wendy went in to talk over some details of the Octoberfest with Mrs. Johnson not knowing that JD had stopped as he heard her go in and had retraced his steps to listen at the door.

"Hi Mrs. Johnson, are we almost ready to go?"

"We're on our way, Wendy. You've done a real good job. You should be proud of yourself."

"Hey! Who picked up the decorations? And who picked up those plates, table cloths and silverware? Things keep showing up around here and I don't know how they get here."

"Oh, I had that arranged." At the door, JD had to smile at that response.

He heard Wendy speak again, "What about the booths?"

"I think I can take care of that. You don't need to worry about it."

"Whew! Good! I thought I might need the football team to set those heavy things up! I think we've got everything taken care of except the clean up crew. No one will sign up for that."

At that JD left. He smiled to himself. He must remember to tell Mrs. Johnson that he would have a crew ready to clean up next Saturday night. As he made his way to the car he reflected on his past week. He seemed to never have been busier, but he'd had fun. He had worked hard all week in practice, but he still didn't think he would play that night. He had worked on his studies, and started to raise his grades. And he had been helping Mrs. Johnson when she needed it. He couldn't help but be pleased with himself. Now if only he could get in the game tonight!

CHAPTER 10

A cold October breeze blew across the brightly light-ed home field as Fort Sage warmed up before their first league game that night against River Bend. JD felt River Bend would not be as easy a team to beat as Twin Buttes. They had a veteran senior quarterback, a speedy halfback, and a solid defense. Still, the home crowd expected victory, especially after last week's win, and the home stands were sure to be full again. As JD threw passes to the receivers, warming up his arm, he looked for his mom and sister in the stands. When he found them at the 35 yard line, he saw them wave and gave a slight wave in return. It made him feel good to see them there even though he didn't think he would play since coach had kept him down on the second string all week.

When warmups finished, the team returned to the locker room for coach Mac's final words, then hit the field for the national anthem, blasting through the sign held up by the cheerleaders. They wore their coveted royal blue jerseys and yellow gold pants. Facing them were the River Bend Bulldogs in their red helmets, white jerseys with red numbers, and gold pants. The team was up, excited. JD was too, even though his excitement was tempered by the fact that he was riding the bench again. He watched as Josh and Hector, the game captains, called the coin toss in the middle of the field, and saw the referee indicate the Wildcats would kick off to begin the game.

He bounced up and down on the cold sideline as the two teams lined up for the kickoff. As Hector approached the ball for the opening kick JD could hear the home fans in their long "Ahhhhhhhhhhhh" that they did before each kickoff. He had noticed last week many sounds he normally didn't hear when playing.

The River Bend deep back caught the kick at the five yard line and headed straight up the field behind a 5 man wedge. But River Bend wasn't holding anything back in this first league game. At the last instant before being tackled the back suddenly stopped and lateralled across the field to his right! The Fort Sage kickoff team was caught totally off guard! The River Bend back that received the lateral took off straight down the visiting sidelines and looked as if he would score. Only Skipper, the safety valve on the kickoff team, had a shot at him. As the home crowd groaned and the visiting crowd squealed and screamed, the River Bend back ate up huge chunks of yardage, running past the 40 yard mark, the 50, the 40, the 30 before being bumped out by Skip at the Fort Sage 25 yard line!

"Way to go Skipper!! Come on defense, let's go," shouted JD at his teammates as they jogged on the field. 'Boy, what a way to start a game,' was what he thought.

River Bend was in great position with a first down on Fort Sage's 25 yard line. On first down they tried a slant off tackle to the offensive right side for a gain of three yards. On second down the River Bend quarterback handed off again to his right on a blast to his I back running behind the fullback. The River Bend I back busted through the defensive line following his full-back. Josh, the Fort Sage linebacker on that side, was knocked aside by the leading fullback and the speedy Bulldog halfback darted into the secondary. The visiting crowd roared as the back ripped off 13 yards before Skip brought him down on the nine yard line, where it was "first and goal".

Having been successful running to their right they again dived off tackle on that side, only to be stuffed by Scott, Fort Sage's big tackle, for no gain. On second and goal at the nine, River Bend tried to counter back to the left with their I-back after faking to the fullback off right tackle. Pete, the Fort Sage linebacker on the right defensive side, stayed home and stepped hard into the hole and dropped the halfback for a 2 yard loss! The home stands jumped and yelled their approval as did the entire Fort Sage bench. Faced with third and goal on the 11, River Bend now faced a passing situation. Coach Roberts, using hand signals to relay the defense to Josh, who called the defensive huddle, gambled and called a blitz with Josh looping outside Scott as he slanted into the middle. The River Bend quarterback called the play in the huddle and brought his team to the line. As he called his cadence Josh jumped up close to the line of scrimmage hardly containing his desire to rush.

The experienced River Bend quarterback recognized this and audibled a "drag pattern" to his tight end. He then barked out loudly "HUT, HUT" taking the ball that the center slapped into his hands and quickly dropped two steps back. He looked for Josh to blitz and saw him coming. This opened up the Josh's area for the drag pass to the tight end and the River Bend quarterback jumped up in the air and fired the ball over the defense's hands right into the tight end's chest. He caught it in full stride and headed up field toward the goal line! Pete, the left side linebacker dove for his feet but missed and only the Fort Sage secondary had a shot at him. Skipper, and Ross, playing JD's monster slot, converged on him from both sides and brought him down with a touchdown saving tackle on the one yard line!

Faced with a 4th and goal from the one, the River Bend coach called time out to go over his options. Mac and Coach Roberts talked on the sidelines before Coach Roberts went out to meet the team at the hashmark.

"Do you think they'll kick it Mac?"

"Heck, I don't know. If they line up to kick, let's try to block it. But I'm guessing they'll go for the TD."

"You think they'll try off right tackle again?"

"Well, they might, they ran there 3 times in a row. But I'm thinking they might try to pop their tight end again on that 'drag'. The scouting report said they ran a roll out option in this same situation last week; they might try that."

"Alright, I think we better have our end stuff that tight end hard and tell the corners to be ready to come up hard in case they run an option: that is, if they come out and go for it. If they kick we'll come like gang busters. Sound good?"

Coach Mac sighed. A coach never really knew what the other coach was going to call and all you could do was make your best guess and hope the kids could come through. "Yep," he said with tight lips, frowning in thought. Coach Roberts started to run out on the field, but Mac called him back on a hunch. "Tell Wilson to stay back and watch for a fake if they line up to kick." Coach Roberts hurried out to make the adjustments with his goal line defense.

After the time out, the River Bend offensive team broke the huddle at the hashmark on the visiting team's sideline, ran to the line of scrimmage and lined up for the field goal. The Fort Sage defensive line dug their cleats in the turf to get some traction. They wanted to block the kick and they were all coming! That is, everyone except Skipper who stood as a safety, right in the middle of the end zone.

As Skip watched, the River Bend quarterback, who was the holder, set his hands and the center sent the ball spiraling into them. The soccer style kicker stepped into the ball with a strong swing of his leg and missed! But no! The holder jumped up from his down position, whirled in a circle and sprinted toward the right side of the field. Skip looked for possible receivers and saw the tight end on the kicking team releasing into the right flat, the corner of the end zone.

"Fake! Fake!" he found himself yelling as he sprinted to cover the tight end. "Get the quarterback!" Paul, the defensive end on the left side, had madly rushed toward the kicker and now he had to swerve toward the running quarterback to try to cut him off from the end zone. The River Bend quarterback could try to run it in or try to throw it to the tight end in the corner. He stopped and set his feet to throw as Paul and Josh turned and bore down on him.

'If he throws it to the tight end, I've got it!', thought Skip to himself as he drove hard at a spot just in front of the tight end's shoulder in order to intercept. Then the quarterback did something totally unexpected. He threw the ball all the way back across the field toward the left end zone corner.

"What the?" said Skipper as he jerked to a stop and turned to look at the opposite corner while the ball sailed high over his head. There, standing in the end zone was the kicker!

"Oh no," groaned Skip out loud. Then he watched the ball settle softly in the kicker's hand and heard the visiting stands erupt in cheers as the back judge signaled touchdown!

Wary of another trick play on the extra point, the Wildcats didn't rush as hard and the kick was good. In just a few short minutes in the first quarter Fort Sage was down 7-0 in their first league game.

After the touchdown, coach Mac called his kickoff receiving team together and exhorted them to get a good return. He knew it was important to get something going quick before his team lost all momentum. Skip was able to return the ensuing kickoff back to Fort Sage's 35 yard line, and it was here that the Wildcats began their first drive.

Mac had sent Bobby with the first two plays, both runs. The team broke the huddle with a loud clap of their hands and Bobby barked his signals. He took the snap and spun to his right, slapping the ball into Pete's stomach as he dove straight between the right tackle and guard. The Fort Sage line surged forward and the home crowd cheered when Pete gained 5 yards. This had the effect of picking the team up a little after being down from the early River Bend score.

On second down the team came out in an "I" formation, double tight end set with Skip playing a flanker slot on the right side. As Bobby barked signals, Skip ran in motion to the left side. Just as he reached the tail end of the offensive line the ball was snapped. Bobby did a reverse pivot and handed off to Ross on a blast off left tackle. Skip turned upfield and kicked out the left cornerback. The Fort Sage tight end blocked down on the defensive tackle and Pete led Ross through the large hole that had been created, knocking the River Bend outside linebacker to the side with a shoulder block. Ross burst through the hole and cut outside toward the left sideline, away from the River Bend safety and gained 12 yards before he was knocked out of bounds by the River Bend free safety.

"Alright!! Way to run Ross!" Pete said as he smacked him on the shoulder pads when he returned to the huddle. The team was now getting pumped up after two straight successes and the home crowd was yelling. With the ball on the River Bend 48 yard line, Mac called Pete's number again, only this time to the left. Pete bulled through the line for 4 more yards.

On second down and six from the 44 yard line, Mac tried Pete again on the right side, on a straight dive out of a split back formation, but the River Bend coach was now pinching his tackles and Pete was met hard at the line of scrimmage for no gain. Now Mac was facing a predictable third down passing situation, something he did not like to be in. He had not thrown much in the last 3 games simply because of Bobby's erratic arm. He called for a quarterback draw on third and six. Bobby called his signals at the line, took the snap and dropped back in the pocket as if to pass. River Bend had expected a pass and had blitzed two of their three linebackers. The Fort Sage offensive line was able to pick up the 5 rushing defensive linemen but not the two linebackers. Bobby saw as he dropped back that the draw wasn't going to work and looked for some way to get out of the pocket. He stutter stepped twice to his left then back to his right and was hit hard for a six yard loss back to the fifty yard line!

Feeling exasperated with a fourth down and 12 facing him Mac sent in the punt team, then called Skip over to him on the sidelines.

"Wilson, when you get into the huddle, tell 'em I want to run the fake."

"Now coach? We don't have JD punting," said a surprised Skip. "You think we can complete the pass?"

"Yes now, darn it! We've got to get something going. Now get out there!"

"Right coach," said Skip as he sprinted back to the huddle.

"Two can play this trick game," Mac muttered under his breath. Few people had noticed Mac and Skip talking, so when the ball was snapped to the back up punter and he threw a wobbly, almost too short pass to a wide open Skipper twenty yards downfield on the right side, it was a real surprise. If Skip hadn't had to wait for the ball to come to him, he would have scored easily. As it was, he was tackled after only gaining an additional 5 yards. Still, Fort Sage now had the ball on the River Bend 25 yard line!

"All right! Good catch Skip! Way to chuck it Gene," yelled JD and his teammates on the sideline as the team ran forward to huddle.

Coach Roberts smacked Mac on the back and said excitedly, "Good call, Coach, good call!" Then he tapped his headset and continued, "George says he can see from the booth upstairs that they are loading up the line of scrimmage on first and second down. We need to throw on first down."

Mac considered that for a moment then sent his guard in with another running play, a blast out of the I-formation off tackle behind Scott on the right. Pete led Ross through the hole for 4 yards. Mac then sent Pete straight up the middle on a quick dive, again out of his double tight end I formation. Pete hit a crack in the line between Josh's block at center on the Bulldog noseguard and the right guard's block on the middle linebacker over the center, and charged past the line of scrimmage. He was hit high on the shoulder pads by the River Bend left linebacker, bounced off and spun in a circle, still lunging forward, gaining yards with every step. The River Bend safety, shrugged off Skip's downfield block and came up to make the tackle, hitting Pete hard with his shoulder in the middle. Pete, was knocked sideways by the hit, but still kept pushing with his feet as he began to fall. The River Bend left cornerback drove him hard into the ground after he had gained 13 yards!

The Wildcats now had first and goal at the eight yard line. Pete bounced up from the tackle and ran back to the huddle even though he had taken two hard shots. He never wanted an opponent to know he was hurt. The crowd loudly cheered his display of eagerness.

On first down, Mac spread his offense with two wide outs, a flanker to the right and split backs. He tried a straight dive to Ross on the left side, but he was stopped cold at the line of scrimmage. A second down plunge with Pete on the right side out of a pro set formation moved the ball to the 4 yard line.

On the sideline Mac again felt frustration building in him. He hated being in situations where passing was pretty much necessary, but he preferred to keep the ball on the ground as much as possible. Usually he would only have a few seconds to think about what play to call as he never wanted to get a delay of game penalty. He glanced at the game clock and saw that only 15 seconds remained in the first quarter. "Good!" he said, "We'll just let that run out." He called Bobby over to the sideline, as the time ran down on the first quarter.

As the two teams changed ends of the field Mac went over his options. He could send Pete banging into the line again, but the other team was probably expecting that and would be in the gaps in their goal line defense. He considered a sweep, but recalled the old saying 'the shortest distant between two points is a straight line', and decided against it. Coach Roberts was urging a pass to Wilson on a quick slant pattern. Mac did not go with that suggestion either. Mac decided to go with what he considered his strength. He had already decided to go for the TD if they didn't score on third down, as he wanted to keep the momentum. As the ball was being marked ready for play he gave Bobby his instructions.

"Alright Bobby, call two plays in the huddle. Let's run I formation, double tight ends, flanker left, dive right with Pete. If that doesn't score, don't call time out, just get up to the line quickly and run the same formation, but the fourth down play will be the counter back to the left with Ross. Got it?"

"Yes, I've got it," Bobby nodded.

"Remember, call both plays in the huddle now. Don't huddle for the fourth down play if we run it. Tell

Josh and Scott we need some blocking!" The referee blew his whistle to signal the ball ready for play and Mac knew the 30 seconds allowed for each play to be run would start. He shoved Bobby by the shoulder onto the field. "Quick now, we don't want a delay penalty!"

Bobby sprinted in to the huddle and gave the instructions, repeating them twice, then broke the huddle and brought the team up to the line. He saw the back-judge glancing at his watch and knew he better hurry.

"Blue! Ready! Set! Hut! Hut!" he called out. The ball came up hard into his hands and he did a reverse pivot to his left and handed the ball off to Pete with his left hand. Pete cradled the ball as he hit the mass of players at the line powerfully, his feet churning. He slammed into the back of his offensive right guard and came to a stop. He tried to slide sideways and turned his shoulders at right angles with the ground trying to slice into a crack and gain ground. It didn't work. The River Bend defense had thrown the offensive line back with a surge as the ball was hiked and Pete was tackled for no gain bringing up a fourth and goal at the four yard line.

The visiting players and fans were celebrating their success after the tackle, shouting and giving high fives and were taken by surprise as the Wildcats lined up to run a play without a huddle. Some of them had assumed that Fort Sage would go for a field goal and they were unprepared for this. As Bobby barked his signals, the visiting coach screamed for a timeout, but his players were running around trying to get in position and didn't hear him in time. Just as Bobby called out the second "Hut" the Bulldog left corner ran to the sidejudge to signal timeout, but the ball was already in Bobby's hands and the sidejudge simply waved him away.

Bobby did the same reverse pivot behind his center, only this time he faked the dive to Pete with his left hand empty, and handed the ball to Ross on the counter with his right hand. Ross took the handoff at full speed toward the right side of the offensive line. With some of the River Bend players not quite in position it was almost easy.

Scott, the big Wildcat tackle on the right side, caved in a half standing Bulldog defensive tackle and Skip plowed into the standing defensive end. Ross hit the hole and ran into the endzone untouched as the linebackers had lunged toward the fake to Pete. The home stands roared as the referee signaled touchdown Fort Sage! Hector's extra point made it 7-7 with a little over 10 minutes left in the half.

Coach Roberts, jumping up and down on the sidelines, popped coach Mac on the back. "Caught 'em off guard twice on that drive Coach! Way to go!"

Mac nodded, smiled and waved him away. He tried not to ever get too excited or too upset on the sideline. He had learned over the years that it unsettled his team.

As the teams lined up for the kickoff, the River Bend coach yelled and complained to the referee that his team had called time out, and that the score shouldn't stand. The referee refused to listen and the River Bend coach became irate, and threw down his clipboard in front of the official. Watching, Mac smiled as the ensuing 'yellow flag' came flying out of the official's pocket. "Thank you very much," Mac said to himself. "Now we'll kick from your 45 yard line instead of our 40."

With the penalty, and a running start, Hector was able to put the kickoff into the endzone, forcing River

Bend to start their next drive at their own 20 yard line. The Bulldogs gained a first down on three plays, but then were held to a gain of only six yards on the next series and were forced to punt. The Bulldog kicker sailed the ball high and out of bounds on the Wildcat 38 yard line, where Fort Sage took over.

The Wildcats couldn't do any better and punted themselves after running only three plays, giving the Bulldogs the ball back on their 29 yard line with 4:52 left in the half. Junking the run, and trying to open it up, River Bend began to use their experienced quarterback's arm. Three sharp passes moved the ball up to the Fort Sage 40 yard where River Bend faced a second and two for the first down. The Bulldog coach tried to go for the score and called a deep pass to his wide receiver on the right side. The Bulldog quarterback took the snap and dropped back into his pocket looking toward his two receivers on the left side. Only when he finished his five step drop did he turn and glance at his receiver on the right, running a deep fly pattern. He thought he could complete the pass in the open area in the Wildcat zone defense between the safety and cornerback. As the Bulldog receiver cleared the cornerback the River Bend quarterback let the pass fly.

It sailed straight and true toward the sprinting wide receiver and he thought they were going to score. He hadn't counted on the closing speed of the Wildcat safety, Skipper, though. As he watched the pass spiral toward his receiver, a blue jersey, in a blur of color, entered his field of vision from the left. Then he saw Skip jump and knock the ball out of bounds just before it settled in the receiver's hands. "Geez! Where did that guy come from?" the River Bend player asked himself. "Man that guy is fast!" The incomplete pass stopped the clock at 2:34.

On third and two from the 40 yard line, River Bend tried to get the first down on the ground with a blast off their right side. Josh, Scott and Paul all converged on the ball carrier and drove him backwards after a gain of only 1 yard bringing up a fourth and 1. After another time out to think things over, River Bend lined up and tried to quarterback sneak the ball over the first down mark, but the quarterback was stuffed hard by the Wildcat noseguard and both linebackers. The referees called timeout in order to measure.

All eyes were on the chain and yard marker as it was brought on the field and stretched out toward the football. The home stands cheered loudly as it showed the football six inches short of a first down. The Wildcat defense had held once again and Fort Sage took over with 1:55 showing on the clock.

On the sidelines coach Roberts urged Mac to throw the ball, but Mac didn't want to turn it over this close to halftime and he was still uncomfortable with Bobby's throwing accuracy. Three running plays gained a first down across the fifty yard line but also ran the clock down to 25 seconds. Mac then tried a reverse to Skip but the River Bend defensive end stuffed him for a six yard loss. After that, Mac had Bobby fall on the ball to run the clock out, much to the displeasure of the home crowd which screamed and yelled for a deep pass. The two teams jogged to the locker room tied at the half 7-7.

In the locker room the coaches quickly asked the players if they had any questions that needed clearing up, then they spent five minutes discussing possible adjustments. All three felt they were running the ball

OK, and that if River Bend came out throwing passes they would have to pressure the quarterback more. Both Coach Archer and Coach Roberts urged Mac to start passing, but he resisted, still not confident with Bobby. After making a couple of defensive changes the team hit the field for the second half.

Fort Sage received the second half kickoff and was able to push the ball up to the visiting team's 48 yard line on eight running plays, but then the drive stalled and they were forced to punt the ball away, giving River Bend the ball on their own 18 yard line.

On the first series River Bend tried to attack on the ground again, and they were able to punch out two first downs in a row and get the ball up to their own 40 yard line. After a dive to the right and one to the left were stuffed for no gain, they faced a third and ten. The Bulldog quarterback was able to put the ball right in the chest of his receiver on a crossing pattern over the middle, but a vicious hit by Skipper jarred the ball loose and River Bend was forced to punt as the clock ticked off the last seconds of the third quarter.

After the 35 yard punt sailed out of bounds the Wildcats took over at their own 25 yard line to start the fourth quarter. On first down Mac tried the first pass of the night, a simple slant to Skip, which Bobby was able to complete for a gain of 8 yards. On second and two Pete plowed over the right side for a gain of three yards and a first down. Mac tried to throw again on first down but Bobby's pass to Skip on a 15 yard out pattern fluttered and was knocked down by the Bulldog cornerback. Facing second and ten, Mac called for a quick drag pass to the tight end. Bobby took the snap, a two step drop then let quickly threw the football to his right.

The Fort Sage tight end was open in between the middle and outside linebackers, but the pass was knocked down by the outstretched hand of the onrushing defensive noseguard. On third and ten Mac called for a screen pass to the right side. It worked beautifully, catching River Bend's onrushing linemen by surprise and Pete gained 25 yards up the right sideline. Unfortunately, the play was called back by an offensive holding call against Josh, the center. After the ten yard penalty, Fort Sage faced a third and twenty at their own 26 yard line. Mac called for a draw to Ross, but he was only able to gain six yards and Fort Sage was forced to punt.

With 9:36 left in the game, River Bend went on offense with the ball on their own 34 yard line. The Bulldog coach decided to go with the passing game and his quarterback was able to complete the first two passes to move the ball all the way to the Fort Sage 45 yard line. The first down pass attempt from there resulted in a sack by a hard rushing Paul for a loss of five yards, putting the ball square on the fifty yard line. Coach Roberts, gambling, called a blitz on second and fifteen, pinching his tackles and looping his linebackers. The River Bend coach called a draw up the middle to his fullback.

The Bulldog quarterback took the snap and dropped deep into his pocket looking to pass. He then pulled the ball down from his shoulder and stuck it in the fullback's stomach who took off straight up the middle.

The Fort Sage linebackers were out of position by the blitz they were in, and the noseguard, tied up with the center could only get an arm on the fullback as he headed up field. The Bulldog fullback powered through that arm grab and cut to his left. Both Skip and Ross had been run deep down field by receivers and the flanker was shadowing Bobby, the left cornerback, as he tried to come up and make the tackle. The Bulldog runner broke it outside and turned the corner around his flanker's block and gained 16 yards before he was brought down hard by a recovering Ross. With the clock running, River Bend now had a first down on the Fort Sage 34 yard line.

A quick slant pass on the side away from Skipper gained nine yards. A second down run was stopped for no gain, but the Bulldogs got the first down on a dive by their fullback down to the Wildcat 22 yard line. The Fort Sage defense, with many players going both ways all game, was beginning to tire and the success River Bend was having was building upon itself, giving the visiting players more confidence with every play. River Bend, trying to avoid a turnover, ran a blast to the left and then to the right, gaining a total of seven yards. On third and three from the fifteen the Bulldog quarterback rolled out to his right on a sprint out pass. Unable to find an open receiver, he barely slipped under Paul's outstretched hand and dove for the first down on a scramble to the eleven yard line!

The visiting fans cheered wildly now, sensing that even if they didn't score a touchdown, their team could win with a field goal. A first down run straight up the middle was stuffed by both Pete and Josh for no gain. On second down, the Bulldog quarterback dropped back to pass and dumped the ball off to his halfback swinging out of the backfield to the right side. The speedy back caught the ball and headed up field, gaining seven yards before being brought down by Josh and the Fort Sage left cornerback on the four yard line! The clock showed three minutes remaining and was running when Coach Roberts asked Mac for a timeout. Mac hesitated, thinking he might need them later, but they had to do something to stop the momentum of River Bend, so he agreed.

Coach Roberts, holding the water bottle rack, ran out on the field to talk to his defense, and try to reassure them, although there wasn't much you could say in a situation like the one they were in. He looked at the hard breathing players with sweat dripping from their noses.

"Alright you guys, anyone need some water? Look, they've got third and three for the first down, four yards for the TD. We've got to hold them and make them try to kick the field goal."

"Yeah, if they kick it," said Skipper, tired and trying to get some air.

"I doubt they'd try that trick again. We'll worry about that when it comes. I want you guys in our seven man gap defense, with our four defensive backs up close. I expect them to try their right side again, they've preferred it all night. You corners and ends watch for counter plays. Now let's go! We can do it!" finished Coach Roberts. He grabbed the water rack and jogged off the field.

With 2:55 left in the game River Bend broke their huddle and came up to the line in a double tight end formation, the ball on the right hashmark. It looked like they were going to run. The quarterback barked his signals, took the snap and whirled to his right faking a hand off to the halfback on that side. He pulled the ball out and bootlegged out to the left with his left halfback leading him. The left tight end had blocked down for one count and then released out into the left endzone corner. The right tight end had released into the middle of the end zone. It was an option pass, only the reverse of what the scouts had seen the week before!

Ross and Skip both reacted well and had the two tight ends covered in the endzone, forcing the quarterback to run. His leading halfback chopped the Fort Sage defensive end and only Bobby remained between the quarterback and the endzone as he sped for the corner. Bobby had dropped back and out to the side as the play had developed.

When he saw the quarterback release and tuck the ball under his arm Bobby came up fast and hard aiming to cut him off before he reached the first down marker. The River Bend quarterback was big and strong. As he ran for the left goal line corner he lowered his shoulder preparing for the shock of the tackle. Bobby was a sure tackler and when he drove into him with a loud smash, the sound was heard all round the field. The River Bend quarterback had neglected to switch the football to his outside arm and Bobby's shoulder smacked the football square and it popped up and back. The momentum of the tackle carried the Bulldog quarterback and Bobby out of bounds at the two yard line and the football bounced lazily around back toward the five, where it was recovered by Ross in a wild dive, ahead of a River Bend offensive back.

The home fans went wild! Their defense had held again! On the sidelines Bobby slowly rolled over and tried to get up, but fell back on his back grabbing his left shoulder. He was hurt.

Time was called as the coaches and team doctor

worked over Bobby. His shoulder pads were removed and the ugly, dangling left arm made coach Roberts's stomach turn. It appeared Bobby had suffered a broken arm or a shoulder separation. The doctor quickly immobilized his arm, then told coach Mac he'd have to get him to the hospital. Mac grimaced when they carried Bobby to the bench to await the ambulance with his parents. He never liked to see any player get hurt.

On the sidelines JD watched with a pained expression as Bobby was set down on the bench. Then it dawned on him that he was the second string quarterback and he began to warm up his arm. He saw Mac and coach Roberts engaged in a heated discussion on the sideline away from the players and as he walked over toward them to get some instructions from Mac he caught the last of it.

"Mac, we have got to have Douglas in there, we don't have anyone else!" said Coach Roberts urgently.

"There's Gene," replied Mac.

"Gene, geez, Mac, he's a sophomore! He's never taken a real game snap!" Coach Roberts almost yelled, his face red. "If we don't play Douglas we will lose this game!"

"Keith!" Mac's voice raised with his anger, his eyes hard, and his voice sharp and cutting. "We discussed this before the game! I told you that Douglas was being disciplined and that's it. Final. End of discussion!" Coach Roberts turned, stuffed his hands in his coat pockets and stomped off. Then Mac turned and looked past JD as if he wasn't standing there and called Gene, the third string sophomore quarterback over.

"Gene, you're in," he said when the startled kid came over to him.

"I am? But. . .But what about JD?" he asked.

Mac looked at Douglas standing next to him, eyes wide in question and consternation, and John could see the conflict in his face. "I'm sorry Douglas," he said quietly, "Gene, you're in there!" Then he turned to Gene and gave him the play he wanted him to run.

As the third string quarterback trotted with weak knees on the field the home stands began to boo. Calls of 'We want Douglas' could be heard all over the home side. John just stood there. He felt angry, confused, betrayed. Hadn't he worked hard all week? Is this how he was to be rewarded? His old surly, smart aleck, attitude began to well up in him. He had the urge to tell Mac just how he was feeling.

JD fought with himself, trying to think clearly. He looked at coach Mac next to him, and heard the booing behind him in the stands as his coach gave young Gene instructions. Shaking his head dejectedly, he turned and walked slowly down the sidelines.

Mac's ears burned with the booing. He knew that both of his assistants were unhappy with him, but he had already made up his mind about this. Now was no time to change. It occurred to him that his mistake had been in not working Gene with the second team all week. He saw JD turn and start to leave. He started to speak to him when his attention was jerked back to the field as Fort Sage broke the huddle.

Gene was nervous, and he didn't think he could even hand off to Pete on the first play. He didn't. He took the snap, turned and tripped over the center's feet and fell down for a two yard loss back to the three yard line. He did a little better on second down, managing to get the ball to Pete on the same dive to the right. That was able to move the ball up five yards to the 8. Facing third and seven, Mac knew he couldn't risk a pass and called for the counter to Ross out of the I formation.

Gene, still nervous, called the signals, took the snap and turned the wrong way making it impossible to complete the handoff or fake. As Pete and Ross rushed past him without the ball he turned and tried to follow, and was tackled for no gain, bringing up a fourth and seven at the eight yard line. The home fans continued to boo as Gene trotted off the field. Mac patted him on the shoulder as he ran past. The clock had continued to run and was down to 1:10 when River Bend called time out in order to save themselves some time to move the ball after the punt.

During the timeout, Mac reminded his players that the Bulldogs would be coming to block the kick and to watch their blocking assignments. Fort Sage lined up in punt formation after the referee blew his whistle to start play. It was obvious the Bulldogs were going all out to block the kick, as they had all eleven men on the line.

When the ball was snapped back to the punter, the Bulldogs ran a set defensive punt block play. Two River Bend lineman drove hard against the offensive center, pushing him to the right. At the same time two other defensive men intentionally drove the offensive right guard to the left, creating a small hole in the middle of the punt blocking formation. The Bulldog safety darted through this hole straight toward the punter. He shouldered aside the block attempt by the halfback and jumped straight up in the air as the Fort Sage punter swung his leg. The ball smacked into the River Bend safety's chest and bounced back toward the goal! It had been blocked! A mad scramble for the ball ensued and it was knocked further into the endzone. Three different defensive and offensive players dove for the ball and it squirted out of a maze of royal blue and white jerseys out of the endzone. The referee stepped in and clasped his hands over his head. River Bend had scored a safety! The home fans stood in shocked silence and the visiting crowd roared.

"Oh, no! Geez!" shouted Coach Roberts on the sideline as he flung his headset down. The score was now 9-7 River Bend and because of the safety Fort Sage had to punt the ball away from their own twenty yard line.

Coach Mac let out a long sigh as his players came off the field with their heads down. He tried to get the kickoff team up, but he saw the fire was out of his team's eyes. Their one hope now was a fumble on the kick.

The Bulldog backs safely caught the punt from the Wildcats at their own 40 yard line and because Fort Sage only had two timeouts left, burned the clock off with one first down against the dispirited defense. The Wildcats had lost the first league game 9-7.

JD shook hands with the rest of his team and then filed slowly off the field with them. Few stopped to talk with their families tonight. He could hear several hostile fans yelling at Mac through the fence. They were all questioning his ability, asking him if he knew anything about football. JD glanced back and saw Mac walking straight toward the locker room with his head up, not acknowledging the taunts. His mother and sister came up to the fence as he neared the end of the field, calling his name. Bitterly disappointed, JD walked over to them.

"Mom, I . . ." was all he could get out of his tight throat.

"I know, I know. I knew what happened would be hard on you. But listen, you can't give up now. Do you hear me? You can't!"

"Mom," said JD, his head hanging, "I just wanted to play. I tried hard in practice all week! I was early to practice, I ran on my own, what else can I do? Coach still didn't put me in."

It was difficult for his mother to know what to say. She was silent for a moment, wishing again her husband was there.

"John, do you think the people who booed were fair to poor Gene and his family?"

JD's anger and disappointment had prevented him from considering that. He thought for a long minute, then answered, "No, no they weren't. It wasn't his fault."

"Whose fault was it then? Was it coach Mac's?" his mother asked pointedly.

JD let out a long sigh before he answered. "No, Mom, it was mine. My fault. But coach is so stubborn. He won't bend an inch!"

JD's mom laughed slightly. "Sounds like someone else we knew, doesn't it? A man of principle, and honor?"

John looked up, realization in his eyes - his dad. Suddenly he thought he understood why coach Mac hadn't let him play. The last of the team filed by as he took a deep breath and seemed to reach a decision with himself.

"Mom, I'm alright now. I gotta go shower OK? See you at home." He waved, turned and walked, with his head down, toward the locker room, carrying his helmet by the facemask. Just before he got off the field, that the same reporter that had interviewed him a week earlier stopped JD and asked him why the coach hadn't let him play.

JD felt his anger rise. "Look, mister, I don't have anything to say to you! You helped get me in trouble in the first place! Coach Mac makes the decisions on this team, and I don't think people are being very fair to him, or to our other quarterback by booing."

"But what about you," the reporter persisted, "is he being fair to you?"

"I've nothing to say to you I said! Now get off!" JD pushed past him and kept walking.

As he reached the locker room door at the side of the gym, Mac came out and stopped him. "Douglas, wait a minute," he said.

JD stopped and looked him in the eye. Only he and Mac were outside.

"I saw what happened over there just now, and I heard what you said, I appreciate it, and so would Gene," said Mac. "It shows. . ." Mac paused searching for words. "Well....thanks."

John didn't quite know what to say. "Ah, it's alright coach."

Mac looked at JD. He saw a very different kid than was there two weeks ago. "Look, Douglas, I don't know if you understand why I didn't put you in tonight or not. But you keep working hard and you'll be alright."

John's face brightened, "Sure, coach. I'll keep after it!"

"Alright, hit the showers," said Mac as he thumped him on the shoulder pads.

Mac waited outside by himself for a few minutes to gather his thoughts. He felt like he had blown the game for the kids and it bothered him. Had he been right not to play Douglas? Was it fair to the other players who wanted to win? Would it have made any difference? Mac felt inside that he had done the right thing, but he knew he faced a tough road ahead now. His team was 1-3 overall, 0-1 in league and every team from now on would be tough, just like River Bend. Central Valley would be tougher! People in town would be calling for his head for sure and his own assistants weren't happy about what had happened.

They played Lakota High next week, which except for Central Valley, was the biggest school they played. Lakota had been picked by some to win the league this year, and Fort Sage had to travel to their field for the game. It wasn't called the 'snake pit' for nothing! Mac shook his head, and walked slowly inside to talk to his team. He didn't want them to lose heart now, they still had a shot. He also had to get out to the hospital to check on Bobby. "Man, what a depressing night," he said to the darkness.

CHAPTER 11

JD was up early Saturday. He wanted to get to work early and talk to Mr. Franklin about borrowing his large one ton truck to pick up the booths for Mrs. Johnson. Mr. Franklin started right in when he came in the door.

"So, what happened to you boys last night, eh?"

JD was embarrassed and didn't know Mr. Franklin well enough to know he was kidding. He didn't know how to respond.

"Well, we, uh, we uh, we lost."

"Lost, with you on the team! Well, I just don't believe it!"

"Well, we did. It was too bad. The team tried real hard. And it was our first league game – we needed to win it."

"Some folks around say that coach of yourn don't rightly know what he's doing."

Now JD started to get angry. His face began to flush. He tried to ignore him and change the subject.

"Look, Mr. Franklin, I was wondering if I..."

"Now, look here kid," Mr. Franklin cut him off, "I was a wondering what you thought about the coach not putting you in the game last night."

Angry, JD said harshly, "Coach Mac is a good man, and I don't think you or anyone else should be on his case. I blew it a week ago and I paid the price. It wasn't coach's fault. It was mine! I'm the one that hurt the team, not coach Mac."

Mr. Franklin saw he had angered JD. He hadn't wanted to, and JD's answer caused him to view the boy with new respect. He put his hands out, waving them downward. "Easy, kid, easy, I'm just pulling your leg some. I've known Mac all his life. I know he's a good man. He worked for me some here when he was in high school."

JD was surprised to hear that; there was so much he didn't know about the old man. He relaxed under Mr. Franklin's soothing tone and apology. Before he could ask for the truck, Mr. Franklin spoke again. "Interesting comment you made about you being the one hurt the team, not coach. When did you decide that?"

In spite of himself JD liked talking to the old man like this, but he didn't know why. He answered, "When my mom made me think about how the entire home crowd was booing Coach and poor Gene as he ran on the field. I realized I was the one who had put them both in this position. Those people should've been booing me."

"Ah, that's alright, kid. Not all of us in the stands were there booing, you know," and he winked at JD.

John smiled. He had developed a real affection for Mr. Franklin. "Say, Mister Franklin, I was wondering if I could borrow your truck next Saturday..." he began, and then he explained the whole situation to him. Mr. Franklin agreed, on the condition that JD get the job done early enough so he could get to work on time!

"Sure thing," said John, then he hustled out to begin his day at the Quick Gas. He was feeling a little better since last night, and was looking forward to eating some burgers with Ross, Scott, Pedro, Gene and Skipper that evening. That was when he was going to get them to agree to help him set up the booths next Saturday and clean up afterwards. He laughed to himself when he thought about the looks they would give him. But he also knew they would help.

JD arrived on campus early Monday to go over the details with Mrs. Johnson about the booths and the clean up crew he knew he could arrange despite some mild protests from Pete and Skip. Then he went by the girl's coach's office to check the girls' volleyball schedule. He had wanted to do something for Wendy's next home game. What he was going to do he wasn't quite sure yet. He saw it was the following Thursday, the week the football team played Horn Basin. "Well," he mumbled, "that'll give me some time to think something up."

After looking at the schedule through the girls coaches' office window JD made his way across campus and upstairs to his first period Biology class to check on an experiment involving photosynthesis he had started Friday. When he walked in he saw Wendy and a couple of her girlfriends over in the corner going over some notes. They looked up when he entered and he smiled slightly and waved a greeting which they returned. He made his way across the classroom and around the lab counter to check his plants. Standing there out of sight, he could hear them talking. "Say, Wendy," said Nancy, "who's been collecting all that stuff for Mrs. Johnson and the Octoberfest? Every time I go in that room there's more stuff, but I never see anyone deliver it."

"I don't know Val and I asked her and she acted like she didn't want to tell us. Maybe it's her husband."

JD had to smile at that. His attention settled on his plants and he didn't listen to the girls until he heard Jo say something about the Homecoming dance. He moved closer to the corner of the counter to hear.

"No," said Wendy "what's up Maria?"

"Oh, go on Maria, tell her," giggled Val. When Maria just smiled, Val went on, "Maria was asked by Hector to the dance Sunday. He texted her a poem! Isn't that great! Don't you think he is so buff with that dark mustache?"

The girls laughed and JD smiled to himself. He'd have to remember to tell Hector at practice. Then he heard Wendy talking to Jeannie and Jo.

"Well, I don't know. No one has asked me. I'd like to go, but . . ." then her voice trailed off.

"Who do you want to ask you? Maybe I can arrange something," laughed Jo. JD leaned closer to the corner; he had to hear this.

"Well," he heard Wendy say, then all he could hear were whispers. He peeked around the corner and saw all three girls look up straight at him. Wendy quit talking and the other girls smiled discreetly, then shook their heads. JD turned red and returned to his plants.

"What did all that mean?" he asked himself under his breath. He tried to return his attention to his experiment, but found his mind wandering back to the question he had heard asked Wendy. Who did she want to go to the dance with? Was it Stan, the basketball player he had seen her talking with recently between classes? It occurred to him that maybe he could talk to Hector, who could talk to Maria, who might find something out for him. As he mulled that long chain of communication over, the first period bell rang and he had to return to his seat to start class. He sat down with a furrowed brow and waited for Mr. Gordon to finish rollcall.

That afternoon in practice Coach Mac called the team together on the chilly field and had them take a knee. The sky was overcast, and most of the players were wearing thermals under their practice jerseys as the Autumnal weather was becoming increasingly colder. "Alright men, here's the score. The doc says Bobby's shoulder is not as bad as we feared. It's severely bruised, but he'll be out 3 weeks at least." He paused, thinking to himself that his players were on the verge of losing hope in their season. He wanted to encourage them, but he never was one to blow smoke. "You men played a heck of a ball game last Friday. We lost, but I'll take the blame for that. There were times when we should have passed and didn't. Right now things don't look too good to you because we're 1-3, and 0-1 in league. But doggonit – we are a good team! That's why this is so frustrating. I don't want you to get down on yourselves. We've got 5 league games left. If we win 'em all we'll be co-champs."

He could see by the look in his players' eyes that some of them hadn't thought of that fact. "Now, we don't want to start polishing trophies until we earn them – we are going to go through the rest of the season thinking about only the next game in front of us. This week it's Lakota. I'm not going to sweet talk you, they're tough. But we can beat them. We have the ability. All I'm asking of you men is five more weeks of hard work, one week at a time. Can you men do that?"

Mac stopped and searched the young faces. This time there wasn't any loud yelling or clapping, but he could see that each player was thinking seriously about what he had said and they all were nodding their heads in a silent 'yes'. "Good! We'll start right now running offense. Douglas - get in there at quarterback and let's see if we can get this offense going!"

The words made JD almost burst with excitement.

"Yes Sir!" he practically yelled. No one had grumbled about his promotion to first string, in fact some of the second stringers he had worked with for the last two weeks were excited about it. He knew it was up to him to not let his team down; this was his chance. He had to show them that he had truly changed. He led the team through one of their better practices all year that day and when it was over he couldn't wait to get home and tell his mom.

He showered quickly, said good-by to Skip and Pete, who always took their time showering, and made his way out of the steamy locker room. Gene caught him at the door.

"Hey, JD!? Wait up!" John stopped and when Gene came trotting up they left together.

"What's up Geno?" JD asked as they walked through the chill, twilight air.

"Ah, well, Coach Mac told me what you said to that reporter Friday night, how you kind of stuck up for me. I just wanted to say thanks, that's all."

JD was a little embarrassed. He stuffed his hands in the pockets of his blue and gold letterman's jacket. As he walked a few steps he was thinking. Gene was younger and a little smaller than him and he knew the younger player kind of looked up to him. He wanted to say the right thing. "That's alright Gene. Those people weren't being fair to you. And that guy was just looking for another story."

"Yeah, well, I appreciate it, you know? Some of the guys on the team have noticed how hard you're trying. We're kinda glad you're in there now."

"Thanks, Geno, I was acting pretty dumb for awhile there. I just hope I don't let anybody down." He stopped at a street corner where he had to turn for home. He patted Gene on the back and said to the thin, spindly legged quarterback, "You'll get your shot Gene, don't worry, you're going to do alright. Well, I gotta go —see ya tomorrow!"

"Yeah, me too. Thanks, see ya."

JD made his way home feeling better than he had in a long time. He remembered how he had called Gene and the others 'losers' a few long weeks ago – how could he ever have done that?

The rest of the week passed quickly for JD. He finished up a few small items for Mrs. Johnson after practice on Tuesday, and on Wednesday he had a blast playing his monster slot on the first team defense. He asked Hector to see if he could get him some info on Wendy and the homecoming dance, but as of Friday he hadn't heard anything. Practice had gone well all week and he was looking forward to starting his first game.

The team bus pulled out from the gym at 4:30PM for the long ride to the Warriors' field. Mac, sitting up front, reflected on the game's importance. The town big-shots were again calling for his release, only now they didn't want the school board to wait until the season was over! The newspaper had run another article on Thursday questioning his decision making, especially not playing young Douglas after Bobby had been in-jured. For the first time in his career Mac was starting to really 'feel' the pressure of his job. He didn't like it. He considered himself a teacher of young men. Besides, he sure wasn't being paid enough to put up with this garbage. He knew this was going to be a rough game for his kids. The Lakota Warriors had been picked to finish either one or two in the league this year and many figured they were the one team that could beat Central Valley, last year's league champ. He also felt they had a good shot, especially with Douglas back in there. The way they had played against the strong River Bend team told him that. They were going to miss Bobby's defensive abilities at cornerback. And the thing was - when playing on the Warriors' home field, penalties mysteriously appeared at the worst times. Usually when the visiting team scored or was about to score.

Mac laid his head back on the seat, glanced at the dark clouds out the window and tried to relax. Would more rain come? He decided that in his pregame talk this was the game he was going to ask the kids to win for him. He didn't usually do that kind of thing, but he needed it bad.

CHAPTER 12

The rain began at the end of the first quarter and it came down hard. The field, already wet from a heavy rain two days earlier, was a muddy mess in a few short minutes. The rain pounded the field in sheets. With the absence of lightning the game proceeded, and as the half approached, the Warrior players, in their dark red jerseys with black pants, were rapidly becoming indistinguishable from the Wildcats in their gold jerseys and gold pants. No one on the home side objected when the Warrior coach elected to run the half out with the ball on their own 35 yard line by having the quarterback kneel down twice in a row, even though they trailed the Wildcats 6-0.

In the locker room Mac and his assistants were feeling pretty good about things. JD had engineered a first quarter scoring drive mixing some sharp passes to Skip with the running of Pete and Ross. Unfortunately, Hector's kick had veered wide to the right and the Wildcats had missed the extra point. But, with the field now in such terrible shape and the rain continuing, Mac felt that victory was within their grasp. He gathered the team together and told them just that and reminded them of the importance of holding on to the ball in the slippery conditions. Excited about the prospect of beating one of the top teams in the league, the Wildcats eagerly hit the field at the end of the half.

Somehow, coach Mac's warning about holding on to the ball was prophetic. As the clock ran down to five minutes remaining in the game Fort Sage found themselves down 14-6, without the ball! Twice in the third quarter the Wildcats had fumbled, and the second time the Warriors had recovered on the Wildcat 28 yard line and punched it in for a score. Then, down 7-6 and trying for a first down on third and long, JD had thrown an interception! The wet football had slipped off his fingertips as he tried to throw an out pattern to a wide open Skip on the right sideline. The defensive back covering had snagged the ball and ran the 30 yards down the sideline into the endzone for the score.

Now, with rain continuing to fall, the defense huddled on what used to be the fifty yard line. JD anxiously glanced at the clock. He knew they had to have the ball soon if they were to have any chance of scoring. They had used up one timeout earlier in the quarter and now only had 2 left. The Warriors were facing a third and three and John knew they had to stop them here. Feeling bad because of the interception, he exhorted his teammates into stopping the Warriors as Josh called the defensive signals and they broke the huddle.

"Come on guys, we've got to stop 'em here! Now!" said JD forcefully. They could hear Coach Roberts yelling from the sidelines.

"Let's go defense, we need that ball. Scott, watch off tackle! Josh, you and Pete have to come up hard!"

The Warriors broke their huddle and lined up in a double tight end, power I formation to the right. Their quarterback barked his signals, took the snap and handed off to the I-back off right tackle. The Warrior tight end on that side double teamed down on Scott, the Wildcat defensive tackle. Scott, feeling the outside pressure, went down on his right knee and grabbed the offensive linemen's waists, trying to clog up the hole. At the same time, seeing the double team, Paul the Wildcat defensive end, drove hard down the line into the two onrushing lead backs. The collision and the mushy, rain soaked field, caused all three players to lose their footing and fall to the ground. The I-back tried to jump over the resulting pile up but was met hard in the air by Josh, the Wildcat linebacker, and he fell down after only a short gain. The referees brought the chains out to measure, since there weren't any yard marks visible in the slop, and determine whether or not the Warriors had gained a first down. That was lucky for the Wildcats, as it stopped the clock at 4:25.

Facing a fourth and 1 and a half yards for the first down, the Warrior coach decided against chancing a punt in the wet conditions and called another running play to try for the first down. With the clock running after the measurement, he figured he could at least burn more time off the clock if they didn't get a first down. Lining up again in a power I formation the Warriors tried to counter back to the left off the same play they had run earlier. It didn't go anywhere, as Scott and Pete stuffed the I-back for a loss of at least two yards! The defense jumped up and down and the few visiting fans were cheering when JD saw the yellow flag!

He ran over to the head referee, asking what the call was.

"Offsides, defense," replied the ref.

"What?" JD asked incredulously. "How can you call that? Who was offsides?"

"Get away from me son, unless you want 15 more yards tacked on!" the ref said sternly as he walked away from JD to signal the call. Josh, one of the senior captains, came up and pulled JD away from any further protest. He still had his own doubts about Douglas's 'turnaround'.

"Get away Douglas! We can't get another penalty on top of that. What's wrong with you?"

"That guy's nuts, we were not offsides!" JD angrily said.

"You aren't going to change it, just shut up and get back to the huddle," and he roughly pushed JD away.

Coach Mac wasn't as easily buffaloed though. He demanded from the sidejudge to know who was offsides. When told it was 'number 80', Mac replied that number 80 wasn't even in the game!

"Well, it's kind of hard to see numbers out here with all this rain you know," said the sidejudge, "now get back off the field before you get 15!"

Incensed, Mac had no choice but to keep quiet.

The Warriors then had a first down on about the Fort Sage 45 yard line with only 4 minutes remaining and the clock running. After their first down run was stopped for no gain, Mac signaled for a time out to stop the clock. A second down run was stopped after a gain of only 2 yards and after his Wildcats stuffed the Warrior I back for a loss of 1 on third down Mac called for his last time out to stop the clock at 3:05.

On fourth and nine the Warrior offense again lined up as if to run the ball, only this time their I-back took three quick steps back and one to the side before the ball was hiked. The center snapped it between the quarterback's legs back to the I-back who pooch kicked down the field. The Wildcats, caught at the line of scrimmage anticipating a fourth down play, could only watch the ball sail over their heads and land in the middle of a large puddle of water at the 24 yard line. It was there, with less than three minutes remaining in the game that the Wildcats took over, without any timeouts left. It was going to be their last shot - JD knew.

He hurriedly gathered his teammates in the offensive huddle. He wanted to line up and get the play off just when the referee signaled the ball ready. Realizing time was short Mac had sent the offensive guard running in with two plays for JD to call in a row. The second play was to be run without a huddle. JD explained the call to his offense and quickly broke the huddle. Time was also their opponent now. As soon as the referee stepped back from the ball and blew his whistle signaling it ready for play JD began to call his signals. He purposely did not look to his right, where Skipper Wilson had lined up wide. As he took the snap he dropped quickly back into the pocket created by his linemen, still looking at the split end on his left.

He almost stumbled as the wet, soggy turf seemed to grab at his feet. After a count of two he turned back to Skip, who had run a post pattern, saw that he had a step on the defensive back, cocked his arm and threw. The football sailed straight, with a tight spiral, 20 yards downfield.

Skip cradled it in his hands and ducked as he was hit by the defensive corner and safety. Fort Sage now had a first down on what used to be the 46 yard line!

"Get on the line! Get on the line!" JD yelled at his

team through the rain. "Let's go! On the line!" The second play they had called in the huddle was a screen pass to the left to Pete coming out of the back field. It worked perfectly and Pete ripped off 25 yards upfield before he was tackled. The Wildcats were now sitting with a first down at the Warriors' 31 yard line with 2:10 remaining on the running clock. In the huddle JD could see his teammates felt they had a chance, their eyes burned with hope. Trying to cross up the defense, Mac called a draw to Ross on the next play. JD took the snap, dropped back as if to pass and stuck the ball in Ross's stomach. The defense was looking strictly for a pass and with a quick burst Ross was upfield and in the secondary. He slipped, caught his balance and cut back to the right to avoid the linebacker and picked up 12 yards before he lost his footing again in the muck at the nineteen yard line!

JD ran forward calling for his teammates to get on the line when the backjudge came running in waving his muddy, yellow flag. He heard him tell the head referee he had called holding on Fort Sage.

"Ah geez," said JD as he looked at his captain Josh. "Here we go again!"

The penalty moved the ball back to the Warrior 41 yard line and time was running out. The draw had been a good call, but Mac knew the Wildcats had to go deep now that they faced a first and 20 situation. He ran a guard in with two plays to be called in a row. The Wildcats quickly broke the huddle and came out on the first play with a wide out and two flankers left, while Skip was tucked in behind the tight end on the right. On this particular play there weren't any backs in the backfield to help pass block, so the risk of a sack was great. Skip was to follow the tight end straight up the field 10 yards and then break out and up while the tight end broke his pattern back to the middle.

The Wildcats had two things going for them. The onrushing defensive linemen were having a hard time with their footing and the Wildcat receivers knew where they were going while the defensive backs didn't. Consequently, when the receivers made their cuts it was harder for the defense to react. With the clock running JD called his signals and took the snap, dropping back as quickly as he could on the muddy field. Two defensive linemen slipped and fell at the snap of the ball, giving him some more time. As he looked downfield through the rain, he shifted the soggy ball in his fingers, trying to get a good grip. He saw two of his receivers on the left side break into their routes, while one slipped and fell face first.

He bounced on his toes as he watched Skip break his pattern out to the sideline then back up the field toward the endzone. When Skipper cut straight up the field the defensive back covering him slid in the mud and Skip was now ahead of him by two steps. JD could see the Warrior defensive end bearing down on him from his left, and he readied the football in his hands to throw. Holding on as long as he could to give his receiver a chance to clear the defensive safety, he finally threw the football as hard as he could downfield. Just as he released the ball he felt the Warrior defensive end's helmet smack him square in the back and he was driven face first into the brown ooze that was now the field.

JD didn't see the ball sail high, with a wobbly spiral right into Skip's hands at the 10 yard line, but he knew the Wildcats had scored by the reaction of his own sidelines. He pushed himself up out of the muck, wiped the mud out of his eyes and looked for penalty flags. There weren't any! With a little over a minute to go the score now stood Warriors 14, Wildcats 12!

JD jogged quickly over toward his bench to get the two point play from Mac. For a couple of seconds coach Mac debated with himself between running Pete up the middle or trying a pass. JD suggested a naked bootleg out to the left, but Mac told him to keep quiet, he didn't need any suggestions. As the referee blew his whistle signaling the ball ready for play Mac told JD to run the option pass to the right. JD hurried to the huddle and called the play.

"Alright, guys, this is it. We gotta have these points. I formation, option pass right. Everybody got it?" When his teammates nodded, he said, "OK, we can do it now! On two, On two, Let's Go! Ready. . ."

Then the fired up offense shouted "BREAK!" as one and ran up to the line. With rain pelting his helmet, JD called his signals. His wet uniform felt like an additional 25 pounds was hanging on his body, dragging on his throwing arm. He barked his second "Hut", took the snap from Josh, turned and ran down the line to his right. Pete, the fullback, chopped the feet of the defensive end, and Ross led JD out around the end of the line. The Fort Sage tight end was releasing into the far right corner of the end zone, but he was well covered by the Warrior defensive back. Skipper was running across the end zone middle, looking for an open spot. Three other Warriors were coming down hard on JD and Ross as they continued to run out to the right side. Ross put his shoulder into them and took out one.

Without anyone to throw to JD tucked the ball under his arm and headed for the red marker standing at the corner of the goal line. Looking to cut sharply upfield, he slipped, then regained his balance. That had slowed him down and now he didn't think he was going to make it!

As the two Warriors angled over to tackle him he jumped in the air, sticking the ball out with his hands, trying to get it over the line. For a brief second, JD seemed to hang in the air as the first tackler hit his legs lifting them up higher than his head. The second tackler tried to hit him square on the shoulders, but since JD had turned when he jumped his body glanced off the Warriors' pads. The first thing to hit the ground were his arms, and they were cradling the football. They landed just across the goal line in front of the red, rectangular goal line marker, while the rest of his body came down behind the line with a big splash and spray of water. JD rolled over on his back searching for the side referee's signal. Standing over him was the same linesman that had called the disputed offsides four minutes ago. His hands were raised up signaling the two point conversion good! The score was tied!

As JD jumped up and was hugged by his teammates he heard the linesman tell the head referee, "Heck of a play 23 just made wasn't it!"

With less than a minute left after the kickoff the Warriors weren't able to get anything going and the game ended tied 14-14. John had asked the refs about overtime, but was told their league only used overtime during the playoffs. On the long ride home in the rain, JD sat up front next to the coaches. Just before he went to sleep, he leaned toward Coach Mac and said, "Well, Coach, sorry we didn't win that one for you."

"That's alright Douglas. You boys didn't lose it either! We played a heck of a game out there! I think we're going to be OK!"

CHAPTER 13

John woke up stiff, sore and sleepy at six the next morning. He didn't remember being this bruised before! Of course, the Lakota game had been the first one he had played both ways all game. He had to get over to the Quick Gas and get the truck, then go get Skipper and Pete and a couple of other football players to help him put the booths up. "Man," he said to himself, "this is getting to be a chore." Still, he was looking forward to completing the project.

After texting Pete, Skipper and the others and rousting them out of bed, JD drove over to the city Chamber of Commerce and picked up the booths. After an hour and a half of good natured grumbling, rehashing of the previous night's game, and work, he and the boys had the booths set up in the park where the Octoberfest was going to be held that night. Then JD swore his helpers to secrecy. They didn't understand, but in the end agreed to go along with what he wanted.

"Hey JD! What are you going to pay us for this?" asked Skipper when they were all finished.

"Well, I, uh, I, uh, well ...." mumbled JD.

"Since you're a working man now, I think you owe us all breakfast! Right Pedro?" said Skip, as he flashed his bright smile.

"Hey! That's a good idea! He got us out of bed early, we're all sore. Yes, breakfast it is!"

"Now wait a minute guys. Hold on. I don't have that kind of cash; I give most of my check to my mom. Besides, you and Pete already got your burgers for this, remember?"

"Hey, I didn't get no burger!" Ross shouted good-naturedly.

"Me either," said Gene and Scott in unison. "Yep, looks like JD's providing breakfast."

All five boys began to chant loudly, "JD, JD, JD!"

It was then that JD saw Wendy's blue mustang turn the corner down the street and approach the park. Oh no, he thought, she must be coming to decorate with some girls. He still did not want her to catch him involved, and he knew once the other guys saw the girls, they'd never leave. Plus, he knew he was stuck for breakfast no matter what. He put his hands out to stop the chanting.

"Alright, Alright, I'll buy you guys breakfast. How about some breakfast burritos at the Burger Bonanza?" He could see Wendy's car getting closer and wanted to leave. "Come on then, get in!" he said as he jumped in the driver's side, started the motor and began to pull away.

"Hey! Wait up man!" called Pete and the other four boys. Pete and Skipper jumped up front and Ross, Scott, and Gene hopped in the back as JD began to pull the faded, white, 75 Ford away from the curb.

"Man, what is your big hurry?" said Skip after he shut the door. JD didn't answer, but burned a 'U' and continued to drive around the park away from Wendy's mustang. As they got on the opposite side of the park Ross began to pound on the side of the truck.

"You two remember," JD said, "you're all sworn to secrecy."

"Hey! Stop! The girls are over there decorating or something! Let's go check it out!" shouted Ross.

"Gotta go to work!" JD shouted out the window and continued on toward the Burger Bonanza.

"What you talking about JD?" said Pete inside the truck. "You don't have to be at work for another hour."

"Hey, do you want breakfast or not?" JD asked. He hadn't told his friends why he swore them to secrecy nor had he told them that he didn't want Wendy to know he was helping with the Octoberfest. He thought about cleaning up that night, smiled and said, "By the way, did I tell you guys about cleaning up tonight?"

Both Skipper and Pete turned to stare and as one shouted, "What?!!"

"Excuse me! Excuse me! Oh no, no way. I have done enough!" said Skip.

"Me too! Absolutely not. I am not cleaning up that mess tonight!" said Pete.

JD just laughed; he knew they would help. He drove on silently smiling. Pete and Skip sat there shaking their heads and grumbling. Then Pete spoke up.

"This is really gonna cost you JD. You know that? Breakfast isn't going to cover it!"

"Say," said Skipper, "Have you told the other three in the back about cleaning up yet?" Then all three laughed loudly.

Back at the park, Wendy and four other girls piled out of her car. Wendy stared after the truck she had seen drive away from the booths. Had they just put them up?

As they unpacked the decorations Wendy asked, "Was that Ross I saw in the back of that pick up?"

"Looked like him," Val answered. "Why?"

"Well, I was wondering if they just put these booths up. Mrs. Williams wouldn't tell me who she had lined up to do it. Who was driving that truck anyway?"

"I'm not sure," said Jeannie, "But it kinda looked like John Douglas."

"I think I've seen that truck over at Franklin's," offered Jo.

Wendy considered that for a moment. She remembered how JD had flatly and rudely refused to help with the festival. Then she thought about how she had bumped into him in Mrs. Johnson's room that morning, how both he and Mrs. Johnson had been sort of evasive. Could he have been behind this? If he was, what was he doing with old man Franklin's truck?

"Nah, he said he didn't want to help with this. It wouldn't have been him," replied Wendy.

JD arrived home after work at 5:15 that afternoon. He had been busy all day and Mr. Franklin had grilled him about the previous night's game again. He had pleased John when he had told him he had played a good game, but he didn't forget to mention the interception he had thrown! He was beginning to think of Mr. Franklin as sort of like a 'grandpa' and he was actually looking forward to talking to him on Saturday mornings.

After showering he plopped himself down on the couch to watch the rest of the ABC football telecast while he finished off a Pepsi and candy bar. He debated with himself as to whether or not he should go to the Octoberfest. He finally decided to head on over there about an hour before it was over and then hang around and clean up afterwards.

After dinner, JD's mom called him in the kitchen to talk to him while she did dishes. She had been very pleased with him lately and she wanted him to know it. She also wanted to talk to him about Wendy, as her mother's intuition told her something was still bothering him.

She looked over at him when he came in the kitchen and sat down on the small table by the refrigerator then turned her back on him to finish the dishes. "John, you played a pretty good game the other night," she began.

"Thanks mom, but I blew it when I threw the interception!" he replied as he lightly smacked his hand on the table.

"Well, you're not always going to play a perfect game, you know. Besides, you saved the game with your dive for the two point conversion."

John blushed under her praise. He never failed to be surprised at her grasp of football. "Yea," he said glumly, "but now that we've lost one league game and tied one, we don't have much of a chance at the title. Even if we beat Central Valley, they'll still be first if they don't lose anymore games."

"Oh, you never know, they might lose to Lakota or River Bend. The season's not over yet! Don't lose heart. Besides, is this only about winning and losing? I think you should be having fun. Winning isn't everything."

"I know Mom, but winning is a lot more fun than losing!" he said with a smile.

His mother continued, "I've been real proud of you lately John. I know you've tried real hard and you went out and got a job! Mrs. Johnson told me at the market today what you've been doing for her. I think that's great, but it seems as if something is still bothering you. Can I help?"

JD sat quietly for a few seconds. What was his mother getting at? Should he tell her about how he didn't know what to do with Wendy? "Ah, well, I'm O.K. Mom."

"What about Wendy? You never brought her over to see me you know. Everything OK there?" From their emotional talk two weeks ago, she suspected that he and Wendy weren't seeing each other any longer.

John's draw dropped. His mother amazed him more each day! How did she know these things? He sat quietly not knowing what to say.

"John, have you two had some problems?"

"Mom," he said quietly, "I don't want to talk about it. OK?"

Now his mother knew she was right, but she didn't want to press him, not now anyway. She could see it was bothering him. Now she turned to face her son and look him in the eye.

"OK, but remember, I'm here if you need help, OK?"

John looked up at his mother. "OK, Mom, but don't worry, alright? Look, I've got to go over to pick up Mr. Franklin's truck and go help clean up after the Octoberfest tonight. Gotta go, OK?"

"Alright, don't stay out late. We have mass tomorrow," she said to him as he headed out the back door.

Wendy arrived early at school Monday morning and headed over to Mrs. Johnson's room to discuss the Octoberfest. As she came down the hallway she saw JD leaving the room and thought she heard Mrs. Johnson call out something about 'thanks - your help'. As she approached JD in the hall she was wondering with what he had helped Mrs. Johnson. As he passed her, JD said "Hey Wendy," and smiled slightly. She thought about letting him go on, but her curiosity was overflowing. Wendy turned around and called after him.

"JD! Wait a minute."

John stopped and turned, not knowing what to say.

"I heard Mrs. Johnson tell you thank you, and I was wondering what you've been doing for her," she said as she walked up to him.

"Well, I had to deliver some stuff for her, that's all. It wasn't any big deal," John said trying to pass it off. He could see Wendy thinking and thought she was going to figure it out. Somehow, he didn't want her to. He continued, "Say, Wendy, the Octoberfest went real well. Seemed like the whole town was there. The decorations were great! You did a great job!"

Since he had rarely done it before, she was surprised at his compliment. Wendy said, "Thanks. Gee, I didn't do it all though. I had lots of help, especially from some anonymous helper Mrs. Johnson had lined up. Seemed like every time I needed something delivered or set up, Mr. or Miss anonymous did it." She stopped and looked at him suspiciously.

"Really?" said JD, "Wow, did you ever see this guy?"

His words startled her. "Who said it was a guy, huh?" she paused, again looking at him with her deep blue eyes, her suspicions rising. "To answer your question, I almost did Saturday. The girls and I showed up to decorate and I saw a white truck pull away with some boys in it. They had just set up the booths. It looked like Ross in the back, but we weren't sure. Then I saw the same truck loaded with bags of trash and the booths late Saturday night after everything was over. I know that whoever was in that truck was my anonymous helper. If I find that truck I think I'll find out who it is." Then she looked straight at him, "You wouldn't know anything about that would you?"

"What me? Nah!" said JD, waving his hand.

"Hmmm, I wonder," Wendy said softly to herself.

"I gotta go see Mr. Quin about a research paper, see you in biology," said JD and he abruptly walked off.

Wendy stood silently and stared at his back. She called after him.

"Hey, JD, I heard you played a good game Friday!"

John stopped walking and turned to look at her, blushing. "Thanks!" he replied. "But all the guys played well." Then he waved again and left.

"I didn't even think she would still care," he said to himself. Yet, her compliment had put a smile on his face. He was looking forward to his first period biology class with her.

CHAPTER 14

At 6:30 AM that same morning Coach Mac was parked at his desk, hunched over his coffee, shivering as he reviewed the scouting report from his freshman coaches. His dingy, little, corner office had never had a heater installed although he had requested it year after year. As he read through the reports again, he had the feeling that the Horn Basin Eagles would be a much easier game for his team than the last two. They were small on the line and their offense had generated few touchdowns in the Eagles' first 5 games. As he looked over the notes one last time Mac became more confident of victory.

Since league play had started up, he had been watching scores and sizing up the Wildcats' chances. It was going to be tough to claim the league title with one loss and a tie now. His own Wildcats would play their next two league games at home; first against Horn Basin, and then the Yellow Jackets from Wheatland High up north. Fort Sage then would play Pine Bluff on the road, and wind up league against Central Valley at home. As it stood right now, only Central Valley, which had beaten River Bend by three points in a close game last Friday, was undefeated. All other teams had at least one league loss except Lakota, whom Fort Sage had tied the Friday before. Central Valley would play the Lakota Warriors the week before they played Fort Sage. Mac knew the team's chances of a league title now depended on three things. First, River Bend had to lose again in league play, and he figured the Warriors had a good chance of defeating them. Lakota would have to defeat Central Valley, but lose to some other team in league. Then, a Fort Sage victory over Central Valley would guarantee Fort Sage at least a tie for the title with Lakota as both teams would have 4-1-1 league records. If Lakota lost again, it would be Fort Sage's outright. Checking the league schedule, Mac saw that the Spartans had to play the Warriors at Lakota High. They could lose. Fort Sage had a chance! Mac realized the whole scenario contained a lot of 'what ifs', and that the chances of Central Valley losing were slim. But, there was still hope!

Horn Basin appeared to be weak, carrying a 0-5 record. Wheatland also had been rumored to be lacking, having only won one game so far, and being soundly trounced by Lakota High two weeks ago. Pine Bluff was still an unknown, but rumored to be very good. It was obvious that Central Valley was the team to beat. So far the top two teams in league had proven to be Lakota and Central Valley. Mac knew that River Bend and his own Wildcats weren't far behind. It had been a few years since the league had 3 or 4 teams that were able to challenge for the title.

Folks around town were still grumbling. The tie against the Warriors had been better than a loss, but it hadn't really helped the team's chances. He wasn't looking forward to the booster club meeting that night at all. More questions from a bunch of 'Monday morning' quarterbacks! How come those that supported him around town didn't seem to go to these meetings? Didn't these people realize he wasn't trying to lose? Couldn't they see the potential of this team?

His thoughts were interrupted by Coach Roberts entering with a box of donuts. Keith closed the door behind him as he came in and sat down on the beat up couch in the corner of the office, under the cabinet that held old game films, videotapes, and DVDs.

"Geez, Mac, when are you going to get some heat in here? Man it's cold!" said Keith as he snuggled in his coat.

Mac eyed him with a touch of humor. "Talk to the administration. So, where's your twin?"

"Oh, George? Well, I don't know, we planned to meet here at 7:00 today. He's late for some reason, maybe he slept in. I don't know how, with that train going by blowing its horn everyday at 6:00 AM!"

Mac laughed. "Well, have you looked at the tape of Horn Basin yet?"

"Yep, watched it four times yesterday. We should eat this team up. We ought to run all over their defense."

Mac considered that assessment, and although he felt the same way, he cautioned. "Let's not get too confident. I've known their coach for over twenty years, and Kirch will have something up his sleeve for us, believe me." He paused, stood up to help himself to a donut and continued while he munched on an apple fritter. "But, I believe you're right. We should win this game without much trouble." Coach Archer walked in, sleepy eyed.

"Hey! Where ya been?" Mac kidded. "You better have some coffee George, we've got to get practice planned."

George blinked and rubbed his eyes. He took a donut, but refused the coffee. "Mac, I've got an idea for offense," he said slowly, in between bites.

"I'm listening."

"Well," said George as he took another bite. "Good momuts!" he mumbled, then cleared his throat. "Well, I was watching Nebraska on TV Saturday, and I think we could use the option offense just like they do. Douglas would be perfect for it."

"Yea, Mac, George and I talked about it yesterday," said Keith. "Douglas can run, and throw. In fact he's our fastest back. I think George has a good idea."

Mac thought about it for a few seconds. "I don't think halfway through the season is the right time to change offenses guys." He shook his head. "I don't think it would be a good idea."

"Mac," George argued, somewhat exasperated, "He's the best we've got. The option would get the ball in his hands more often."

"Right, and it would add a new dimension for teams to defense us," said Keith.

"And it'll cause us to fumble more," offered Mac. "I think we better ride the horse we've got for now."

Keith and George exchanged glances. Each thinking the same thing. Mac would not take advice from anyone. "Can we at least try it in practice?" asked George.

Mac sighed and rubbed his forehead. These two youngsters would not let up! "Not this week. We just got Douglas in there. Let's polish ourselves and get a league win under our belts. Maybe next week, OK?" He looked up at his two assistants, seeing that they were unhappy. Well, can't please them all the time, he thought. "Now what about practice today?"

On Wednesday JD walked home from practice feeling good about how the week had gone. The team had ran through offense on Monday, getting their timing down. On Tuesday, the defense had prepared for the Eagles' 'run and shoot' attack, and today, after running quickly through offense and defense, the coaches had practiced special teams, adding a fake field goal play. Despite their 1-3-1 record, the team had been upbeat. JD felt he was doing a good job keeping them fired up, at least he was trying to. Coach Mac had talked to them Monday, outlining their chances for the league title, exhorting them to take games on week at a time, to try to be the best they could. Of course, they all had been watching the scores themselves and everyone had already known what had to happen for them to take the league before Mac had explained it. In the back of their minds was the 'Bell Game' with Central Valley. No matter what the coaches said, it was like a weight hanging over them. Fort Sage hadn't won the victory bell in 5 years. Each one of them wanted to get it back.

Tomorrow would be the day, JD thought to himself. Since he couldn't 'anonymously' text Wendy, he was going to slip a card he made with the computer in the library into Wendy's locker after sixth period on Thursday. He had printed out a volleyball with the words 'good luck in your game today' on the card, colored it, and remembering what she had said Monday morning in the hall, he had signed it 'Anonymous' as a clue. She always went to her locker after school, and she would get it just before she dressed out for her game.

He wondered if she would figure it out? He had seen her walking toward the gym with the tall basketball player, Stan, after school all week. The thought that he was too late sobered him. Maybe he shouldn't have remained a 'secret helper' on the Octoberfest! Maybe he shouldn't have been such a jerk in the first place! It had been easy for JD to decide to change the way he had been acting and treating others, but it was hard to know if anyone was noticing. He hunched his shoulders in his letterman's jacket as he turned the corner for home. The weather was turning colder each day. What was that saying his mother had told him? It was a lot easier to build and keep a good reputation than it was to get rid of a bad one. He was finding out how true that was.

His thoughts were interrupted by his little sister Mary yelling his name as she ran to meet him as he came down the block. JD smiled to himself, at least she liked him now. As she jumped into his arms to hug him, JD's eyes misted. He remembered how his sister had done the same thing to his dad when came home from work. 'Dear God, we all miss him so much,' he thought.

The next day, JD counted the minutes in his sixth period English class. When the bell rang, he was the first out the door and he made his way to the group of lockers at the end of the library. As an afterthought, he stooped and picked a small yellow daisy in the planter by the library. When he passed locker 401 he glanced quickly around to make sure Wendy was not in sight, and slipped his card, wrapped around the flower, through the slits in the door. Then he briskly walked behind a nearby tree to watch.

Wendy came around the corner with Maria, giggling over her account of dinner Saturday with Hector. She automatically turned the dial on her locker, mentally going over her subjects to decide which ones she had homework in. She continued to talk to Maria as she opened the locker door. As he watched, the card, stuck to the flower, fell out of the locker and down on the sidewalk next to her right foot.

JD groaned, "Ah, geez! That's it," he said to himself.

"Hey, you dropped something," said Jo and Val who had just walked up.

"I did, where?" asked Wendy, then she looked down at her feet where Maria pointed.

"What's this?" she asked as she picked up the slightly smashed flower and card.

She opened the card and read it.

"What is it?" Maria asked, "Hey? Wendy, what is it?"

"Ah, I don't know. Somebody is wishing me luck in today's game," replied Wendy, puzzled.

"Who?"

"Well, it doesn't say."

"Let me see it," Maria said, taking the card and reading it. "Anonymous. Why would someone sign it that way? Do you think it is from Stan?"

Wendy shook her head. "Naw, he would just sign it. Besides, he is just a friend."

"Yea, but he told Jeannie he would like to be more than that with you. Anyone can see it! Can't you?"

"Ah Maria, quit trying to be cupid," said Wendy thinking to herself. "Anonymous, hmmm, you know, I was just talking to JD this morning about our anonymous helper on the Octoberfest."

As the girls gathered their books and turned to leave, Wendy saw caught a glimpse of JD turning around a tree. She watched it closely, hoping to see more movement. Maria was speaking but Wendy was only getting part of what she was saying.

"....not that self-centered snot. You don't think he did this do you? Wendy? Hey, I'm talking to you girl! What are you looking at?" said Maria, then she nudged Wendy with her elbow.

"Oh, I don't know; I saw JD over there by a tree. He seemed to be watching us."

"Oh come on! You're starting to imagine stuff. Like I said, you don't think that self-centered boy did this? Do you?"

At last Wendy took her eyes from the tree where JD stood. "I don't know Maria. He's not like he was a few weeks ago."

"Oh, please..." started Maria.

"No really," said Wendy, "I wonder...."

As they walked toward the gym, JD saw Wendy take the card and the flower and put them in her blouse pocket, just before Stan joined them. 'Well,' he thought, 'I tried.' He chided himself for not just talking to Wendy straight, but he no longer felt confident about her feelings toward him, and that made him afraid. In a glum mood he made his way across campus to join Skipper and Pete on the way to dress out for practice. 'Maybe I'll send her another one next week, and maybe I'll sign it,' he thought to himself, and felt like a complete idiot.

CHAPTER 15

Two weeks later, JD, Pete, Skipper, Scott and Gene met for burgers on Saturday night at the Burger Bonanza on Main Street. It was becoming a ritual on weekends with the five teammates who had become good friends. JD was glad his job allowed him to not have to ask his mom for money to go out, as the family had very little. They sat outside in the cold, chill, October air, in all their high school athletic glory. The four upper classmen proudly wore their blue and gold letter jackets, and Gene, who ached to get his, wore his Fort Sage Football sweat-top outside his thermal shirt.

As they ate, the 5 boys were reviewing the events of the last two weeks. They were all in good moods. Their coaches had been correct when they told them they were going to beat Horn Basin and Wheatland. Against the Eagles the Wildcats literally ran at will, racking up 21 first downs and 320 yards in total offense. The blitzing, gambling 4-4 defense the Eagle coach had installed to surprise the Wildcats wasn't effective and the game was over at the half, with Fort Sage ahead 28-0. Mac had let the first team play the third quarter and then, leading 35-0, he had played subs the entire fourth quarter. It was a point of self pride with Mac that he had never willingly ran up the score on an opponent. Horn Basin managed to score against the second string defense and the game ended 38-7. Fort Sage had played well in all areas, albeit against an undermanned opponent. JD had thrown for two touchdowns, both to Skip, and ran an interception back for another. Pete had scored twice himself, with powerful running up the middle. Even young Gene, the sophomore, had played well, leading a short fourth quarter drive for a field goal. Then, as if the first league win had jelled the team, they had rolled over the visiting Yellow Jackets 24-0. The Wildcat defense proved too formidable again, holding the Wheatland High team to just 3 first downs the entire game. Offensively, they had scored two touchdowns with the running game, one by their 'raging bull', Pete, one by Ross, and JD had thrown another TD pass to Skipper. The team had squared their overall record at 3-3-1 and their league record was now 2-1-1. They joked and kidded with each other, then became serious when the subject of the league title came up.

"Do you think we've got a shot, JD?" asked Skipper.

"Sure! Look, everything's gone just right so far. River Bend lost to Lakota. They've got two losses now, so they're out of it. Pine Bluff lost a close game to Central Valley two weeks ago and last Friday, like we saw on the news, they beat Lakota on their home field on that fumblerooskie play in the fourth quarter. That was just what we needed! Now Lakota has one loss and one tie, just like us."

"Yeah," said Pete, "but, what about Central Valley? They haven't lost a game yet."

"Right," said JD, "But if Lakota can beat them this Friday, then we can tie for the championship by beating Central Valley ourselves."

"Don't forget about Pine Bluff," said Scott, their big,

quiet, junior lineman, as he munched on his onion rings. "They only lost one game all year, to Central Valley, who is still undefeated. We have to beat them first."

"That's right man. Don't be counting your chickens too fast. Pine Bluff has got a good team," said Ross, who had just parked his truck and joined the group. "And we play them over there!"

"I know, I know, but we can beat them! Man, we are on a roll! We just have to stay focused. We can do it. We beat them and they're out of the race, with two losses."

"But what happens if Lakota doesn't beat Central Valley this week?" asked Gene. "If that happens, we're out of it no matter what, aren't we?"

The other five boys were all silenced by that thought. It seemed to let the air out of their championship balloon. They all looked at each other knowingly.

"Don't think so negatively, Geno!" said Skipper. "We gotta have faith!"

"And a little luck," said Pete.

Their spirited conversation was interrupted at that point by Wendy's Mustang pulling up to the drive through window. Four girls were sitting inside, all laughing and giggling as they yelled "Hi!" at the boys sitting outside.

"Hey," said Ross, always willing to talk to girls, "let's go check em out!"

"Yea, good idea!" said Pete. "Text em. Tell em to join us!"

"Hey, great idea man, do it," said Skipper. "Bring 'em over here. Get your cell out!" Scott, the quietest one of the bunch, didn't offer an opinion, but eyed JD mischeviously.

The idea made JD uncomfortable, but he could see he

was outnumbered. Still he offered a dissenting vote. "Ah, we don't need them over here guys. Leave them alone."

Skip looked at his friend knowingly. As Pete, Gene and Ross walked over to her car, he talked to him. "What's wrong man?" he asked.

John looked over at Skipper. He didn't really know what to say to him. "Nothing Skip, nothing."

"It's Wendy, isn't it? Maybe you should just talk to her, apologize. Set things straight."

As the group approached, JD cut him off short.

"Maybe I will, Skipper, maybe."

The four girls, dressed warmly in jeans and coats, pulled up a chair around the table, Wendy sitting across from JD. He noticed how her blue eyes seemed to sparkle as the lights glanced off them. He felt like she was looking right through him. There was some good natured kidding back and forth as they talked about school, parties, the games they had played, and the homecoming dance in two weeks. Maria had the maddening habit of talking to you while texting someone else.

"Maria, does Hector know you're out running around on Saturday?" asked Skip, flashing his great, big, bright smile.

Maria, who was sort of a feminine activist, came right back. "Hey, get off Skipper! Hector doesn't run my life! Besides, he's away visiting his relatives this weekend." At this, the group jumped on her, "WOA, WOA, WOA!" "When the cat's away, the mice will play!" "Wait until I see Hector at practice Monday!" "I think I'll text him right now!" And then they all laughed loudly. When it had quieted down, Ross spoke up.

"Say, Wendy, you girls did pretty well the last couple of weeks in volleyball. What place are you in?"

"Well, after beating Horn Basin, and Wheatland, we're tied for first, aren't we Val?"

"That's right! We've only got to win 2 more games and we go to the playoffs!" said Val excitedly. "We've got to take first in league. Only first place teams go to the playoffs in our section."

"Yeah, we know, that's why we've got to win league in football."

"But," continued Wendy, "you guys aren't doing so badly either. Your last two games were super!"

"Yea, you guys really stomped on the Yellow Jackets. Great game!" said Jo. "You really played well JD!"

John blushed, "Thanks a lot," he said, "but every one of these guys played well. The whole team played well. They all deserve credit."

Wendy again noticed how JD had deferred compliments to the whole team. He had done that a couple of weeks ago when they talked in the hall.

The boys all kind of puffed up at once. Hearing this kind of talk just made the night that much sweeter.

"Speaking of volleyball," Maria asked coyly, "did you ever find out who sent you those notes Wendy?"

"Notes? Notes? What notes?" it seemed everyone asked at once.

Wendy gave Maria a frown, "Thanks a lot Maria! It was nothing, really."

"Oh no, you're not getting off that easy," said Skip, "come on, fill us in."

JD had not told anyone, so only he was the only one of the boys to know anything about it. He pretended to be in the dark, like the rest, keenly interested in what Wendy had to say.

"Alright," said Wendy. "Somebody put two notes in

my locker wishing me luck on the day of our volleyball games the last two weeks. That's all."

"Somebody?" asked Pete. "Why do you say somebody?"

"All the person signed was 'anonymous', that's all. I don't know who sent them. Do any of you?" Wendy eyed JD closely after she asked her question. All of the boys either shook their head or denied it. She thought she caught a slight smile in JD's face before he looked away. She intuitively thought he had done it, but wasn't sure.

The conversation turned to the homecoming dance coming up in two weeks, and who was going with whom. Pete, Maria and Jo already had dates. Seeing that Val didn't, Ross asked right there in front of everyone and received and embarrassed 'sure' in reply. JD, who wanted to go to the dance with Wendy, more than anything, began to squirm as the questions flew back and forth. He wanted to know if she was going with someone, but he didn't want to hear it with her sitting there in front of him. He excused himself to the bathroom, dumping his food basket in the trash as he left. Skipper watched him go, and slowly shook his head.

"Who are you going to ask Skipper?" asked Maria interrupting his thoughts.

"Oh, I don't know, Maria, some lucky young lady," laughed Skip. "What about you Wendy?" he asked, knowing that JD would want to know.

"Well, I don't have a date yet."

"I know two guys that want to go with her real bad, but she keeps putting them off!"

"Maria!" snapped Wendy, obviously not wanting to talk about it, "Sometimes!" She shivered, then said, "It's time to go girls, I'm cold!"

"Me too," said Val. Then the group broke up as the four girls head toward Wendy's car with the four boys following.

"See ya Monday! Bye!" they called to each other, as Wendy started the car and pulled away.

After dropping her friends off, Wendy was alone with her thoughts as she drove home. Why had JD left when they started talking about the dance? Was he going with someone else? Did she care if he was? Was he the anonymous note giver? Why wouldn't he just talk to her like before? Did she want him to anyway? He seemed to have changed, but had he really?

She was only guessing. Did she want to go homecoming with him? Both Stan and Ralph had already asked her to go; maybe she should accept. But something was holding her back. Totally confused, she parked her car in the driveway, went inside her house, and straight in to talk to her mother.

CHAPTER 16

The week leading up to the Pine Bluff game had been a busy one for everyone. Friday arrived and JD could hardly contain his enthusiasm as he finished off the last question in his sixth period quarterfinal and let out a sigh of relief. He gathered his materials, turned in his test to Mrs. Johnson and sat down to await the bell. He had more than a half hour to sit since others were still taking the test, and he was alone with his thoughts.

The week just finishing had been strenuous. The first quarter officially ended today and the last two days all students had been taking quarter-final exams. The team had begun practice earnestly Monday after school and had continued with spirit and new confidence all week. They had run through the offensive and defensive sets and coach Mac had finally relented to his assistant's pressure and allowed the team to experiment with the option series. JD remembered how the team had difficulty with it at first and then gradually he, Ross, and Pete as well as the offensive line had 'gotten the hang of it.' JD smiled as he recalled how Mac had still not liked it, and was not considering using it that night.

John Douglas was feeling much better with himself. He figured he had raised his grades from one B, 4 C's and one D to at least 4 A's and 2 B's, maybe even 5 A's and 1 B. Tonight they played Pine Bluff. The Wildcat football team seemed to be firing on all cylinders, and they were now playing with confidence. Also, Bobby, their senior all league corner, was supposed to be able to play. JD grimaced with a pang of guilt as he recalled how, a few weeks back, that would not have made him happy. Now, he was glad the team had Bobby back. His job with Mr. Franklin was helping him out with spending money, as well as helping his mom. Everything was going great, except for Wendy. He just couldn't seem to get on the right track with her. He had tried talking to her during the week, but seemed to grasp for words each time and the conversations ended uncomfortably. There was still a barrier between them, something to be taken care of. What was it?

His racing thoughts turned back to football. Their football game that night was only about a 45 minute drive to the east. The game was scheduled for 7:30, so the bus would leave at about 5:00. Everyone knew it was important to win these last two games, and everyone knew the Pine Bluff Vikings would be tough playing on their own field. Their record was 6-1. They were going to be as good as Lakota or better. The bell rang, breaking up his daydreaming and he went home to eat a good dinner before returning to school to dress out. He knew that tonight was the most important game so far this year!

With the recent success of the team, a whole caravan of Fort Sage fans made the trek east to the Vikings' home field that night. This was a key game and everyone knew it. The home stands were full and there were probably a thousand visiting Wildcat fans anxiously awaiting the kickoff when JD and the rest of the kickoff receiving team took the field. The last Friday in October was cold, so cold JD had worn a thermal under his uniform, the long white sleeves showing underneath his yellow gold jersey. Fortunately, only a slight breeze was blowing across the field. JD searched the crowd for his mother and sister without success, but he knew they were there, somewhere. He briefly wondered if Wendy had made the trip.

He watched the Vikings break out of their kickoff huddle and it struck him that their green and gold uniforms looked exactly like the uniforms of the Green Bay Packers. 'Let's hope they don't play like them,' he thought. He glanced over to Skipper on his left at the goal line and gave him a thumbs up, which he returned. In a moment, the referee blew his whistle and the kicker approached the ball.

Fort Sage had been well scouted by Pine Bluff. They knew not to kick the ball to number 23 - Douglas. The kickoff sailed high and left into Skipper's arms at the 10 yard line. The return was set up for the right side line. As Skip broke to his right to get behind his blockers, JD cut in front of him and knocked the first player he saw in a green jersey down with a jolting shoulder block. That gave Skipper a little running room up the sideline, but the picket line let too many Vikings slip through and he was tackled on the 28 yard line.

The Wildcats got off to a quick start, busting off five running plays in a row, moving the ball smartly down to the Viking 42 yard line. On first down at that point, Mac called the first pass play. It had Skip wide on the right side running a deep flag pattern, while the tight end and flanker on the left side did simple crossing patterns. JD took the snap, quickly dropped back into the pocket looking for Ross coming across the middle from the left. His blocking broke down on the left side and he scrambled out of the pocket to his right, while he looked deep down the right side. He saw Skip gaining on the Pine Bluff safety as he planted his feet, squared his shoulders and threw. The football sailed in a tight spiral 30 yards downfield, but about a step behind Skipper. Fearing an interception by the closing green jerseyed safety, JD took off downfield. To his relief he saw Skip wait on the ball and expertly time his jump to gather in the ball on the seven yard line as he was driven out of bounds.

"Alright!" yelled JD as he gathered his team in the huddle, waiting for Mac's play. "Good catch, Skipper, you saved me that time. Alright guys, let's punch this thing in!" He called the fullback dive sent in from Mac and broke the huddle.

The Fort Sage offense broke the huddle with a loud "break!" and hustled to the line. JD barked his signals, took the snap, whirled to his right and slapped the ball in Pete's stomach. Pete lowered his head and plowed into the line behind Smith, his right guard, and Scott at right tackle, for six yards. With second down and goal at the one the visiting stands were standing and cheering; and they erupted as the Wildcats ran the same play to the left, and scored! Hector converted the extra point and the 'Cats were up 7-0 late in the first quarter. 'We've got these guys now,' JD thought to himself as he trotted off the field.

Pine Bluff wasn't going to roll over easy, however. A disciplined team, they took the kickoff and moved slowly upfield. After nine plays and two first downs, they faced a third and 4 with the ball at midfield.

The Viking quarterback called his signals. His offensive team patiently waited for the ball to be hiked on the third "hut" for the first time in the game. On the second "hut!" three Wildcat defensive linemen jumped across the line creating an encroachment penalty, and giving Pine Bluff a first down on the Wildcat 45.

Mixing runs with short passes, the Vikings moved the ball down to the Wildcat 12. In the defensive huddle JD, Josh and Pete shouted encouragement to their teammates, trying to keep them pumped up. A second down run was stopped for no gain, bringing up third and seven. The Vikings tried a pass to the deep left endzone corner that JD knocked down in a collision with the receiver. The home crowd booed and screamed for a 'pass interference' call, but all the refs had left their flags in their pockets. Faced with a fourth and seven, the Vikings kicked a 29 yard field goal to bring the score to 7-3 with three minutes left in the half.

After the kickoff, the Wildcats were able to gain a first down, but then they stalled and punted the ball away from their own 39 yard line. Pine Bluff wasn't able to move against the Wildcat defense and the half ended with the score still 7-3.

At halftime, Mac was optimistic with his team, but he secretly was afraid of the Vikings. He could tell they were a well drilled team. As he led his team on the field after the 15 minute break, he felt it was important for Fort Sage to score first in the second half. He didn't want to give Pine Bluff any momentum at all.

As if the football gods had read Mac's mind, the Wildcats caught a break on the second half kickoff. Hector booted the ball deep to the Pine Bluff five yard line where the Viking deep back fumbled it! Then, in a hurry to pick the ball up, he bobbled it again. By then several Wildcats were bearing down on him, and he was forced to fall on the football at the two yard line!

"Alright! Alright! Now let's go defense!" Mac shouted as the team hit the field. He wanted to keep the Vikings deep in their territory. The fired up defense did better than that. On second down, after stopping the first down run for no gain, Scott shot through a hole in the line and tackled the Viking halfback in the endzone for a safety! In a short minute, the score was now 9-3, Wildcats.

Coach Mac and Coach Roberts congratulated the defense as they ran off the field, slapping the players' helmets.

"Kickoff receiving team, on the field!" shouted Coach Roberts. Then, as they huddled briefly with him, as usual, he gave them the return plan and sent them out. "Let's run this thing back far, guys! We want another score!"

After the quick Wildcat safety, the Pine Bluff players looked shellshocked as they lined up to punt the ball away from their own twenty yard line. JD and Skipper stood together back at their own forty awaiting the kick. Skipper had suggested it at halftime, since it was obvious the Vikings didn't want to kick the ball to JD.

As the ball sailed off the kickers foot JD and Skipper separated. Since he didn't know where to kick the ball, the Pine Bluff punter had tried for the left sideline at the fifty yard line. JD had broken that direction when he and Skipper split apart and he rushed over to make the catch.

He was able to gather the football on the dead run

down the left sideline with an almost clear field in front of him. Most of the Pine Bluff players had converged toward the middle of the field. The poor kick coverage cost them as JD rapidly ate up yards crossing the forty and thirty before he was even touched by a Pine Bluff player. The bump he received on the shoulder by the diving Viking threw him off stride and he began to tip-toe down the sideline. He regained his balance at the nineteen yard line and cut inside the last defender, leaving him grabbing air, then he raced into the end-zone for what he thought was a score! Unfortunately, his dance down the sideline after being bumped had caused him to step on the stripe and the sidejudge was blowing his whistle, marking the play dead on the twenty one yard line while he had been running across the goal line.

As he watched JD make his way back to the hud-dle, Mac was clapping his hands, saying over and over, "That's OK, that's OK, let's punch it in!"

A dive by Pete and a counter by Ross moved the ball down to the nine yard line against the now demoralized Viking defense. Mac guessed the Viking coach would be expecting a run and called a play action 'fade' to Skip in the right corner of the endzone. It worked perfectly, as JD faked a dive to Pete and then softly laid the ball in his hands for the score. After Hector converted the extra point, the visiting stands roared their approval as the offense jogged off the field. In the middle of the third quarter the score now stood 16-3 in favor of their Wildcats.

A good team doesn't quit, and after the kickoff the Vikings proved their worth. Their senior quarterback was able to move his team to two first downs after the kickoff, and that settled his team down. When that happened, their plays became crisper and more disciplined. The Vikings moved down the field once again on a long drive that took up the remainder of the third quarter and part of the fourth. With the ball on the Wildcat 24 yard line, the Vikings again tried a pass into the endzone, where Skipper and the offensive receiver both collided as they went for the ball. This time the penalty flag did fly, much to the pleasure of the home fans.

After the referees marked off half the distance to the goal, Pine Bluff had a first down on the 12. Four plays later, after a close measurement, they had a first down on the two. From there, it still took 4 plunges into the line to score against the tough Wildcat defense. It was only the third touchdown the defense had allowed in league play. The extra point tightened the score at 16-10.

With six minutes left in the game, Mac knew his offense had to move the ball. Pine Bluff could easily win the game if his offense couldn't get it going. The Vikings had just scored and they now knew they had a chance. Their defense would be fired up.

After the kickoff, JD was able to guide the team to three straight first downs and burn four minutes off the clock. They had bogged down at the Pine Bluff 41 yard line, where they faced a third and four. When the Viking coach called his last time out to stop the running clock, JD talked with Mac on the sideline with the team huddled on the near hashmark.

"Let's try that option series, coach, they'll never expect it!"

Mac frowned. "No, we're not ready for that yet," he

answered. When he saw JD frown, he added, "Too risky, we might fumble a pitch or something. No, I want you to run that counter to Ross on the left side. We got big yards on that in the first quarter. Let's go, if we get this first down, we've got he game." With that he pushed JD back toward the huddle as the referee blew his whistle.

Back in the huddle, JD urgently told his team they needed this first down. With it, they could wrap up the game. He could see the fire in their faces and he knew his teammates would give it all they had. He called the play, broke the huddle and led them up to the line of scrimmage. He shouted his signals, which were hard to hear due to the noise of the cheering home fans. As he took the snap he pivoted to the left to fake the handoff to Pete over the right side and then hand off to Ross on the left side.

As he did this, his left foot was clipped by the pulling right guard and he was thrown off balance and began to fall. There was no way he could make the hand off to Ross. 'No, not now!' he thought, angrily. He gripped the ball firmly in his right arm and shot his left hand out to keep his knees off the ground. He was able to regain his balance, but his action had brought him to a complete stop well behind the line! Usually, when a play is busted in football, the quarterback is supposed to carry the ball into the hole where it was supposed to go in the first place. A quick glance at collapsing line of scrimmage told JD that wasn't going to work. There wasn't any hole, no room to run.

Instinctively, he broke to his left, circling deep into the backfield trying to turn the corner. The onrushing Viking defenders cut him off and he cut back to his right, scrambling for yardage. A defensive lineman dove for his legs, but JD jumped over his arms and into a small crease he saw on the right side. His scrambling had caused the players on both teams to get out of position and he now dodged and weaved his way forward, lunging through the arm grabs by the Vikings.

Both the visiting and home crowds roared and screamed as he lunged back toward the line of scrimmage. He was hit on the left hip and wrapped up. Falling, he caught a glimpse of Skipper off to his right side and flipped the ball out to him. He felt a hard smash in his back, which propelled him forward and down. He felt the hard shot in his ribs from the helmet as he smashed into the turf, not seeing Skip catch the ball and lunge forward as he was being tackled by two Vikings.

After the players unpiled, the referees called timeout for a measurement. Everyone in the stands and on the field strained to look at the chain as it was stretched out. JD jumped and pumped his arm as he saw the ball sticking out halfway across the marker. Fort Sage had a first down! With that, the Wildcats were able to run out the clock and seal the victory! The Wildcats had defeated the Vikings 16-10 and they were still in the running for the league title!

The team whooped and hollered, clapping each other on the back as they made their way off the field after shaking hands. Their fans lined the fence around the field clapping and cheering them as they walked down the sideline to the bus. JD, smiling, waved to his mom and sister, then out of the corner of his eye he saw Wendy near the fence, watching him. He stopped and was about to call her name when several players came up and grabbed his shoulders, dragging him along. He looked again and couldn't find her. He smacked hands joyously with his friends Skipper, Pete, Gene, Ross and Scott and several others as they made their way off the field, part of his mind thinking about her.

As he boarded the bus, JD overheard Mac ask the local reporter if he had a score on the Lakota-Central Valley game. The happiness of the victory had caused him to forget about that for a few moments. Now, the nagging thought returned. They still needed help from Lakota.

CHAPTER 17

The following Saturday night, JD met the group - Skipper, Pete, Gene, Scott, and Ross - at the Burger Bonanza on Main Street in what had become a weekend tradition for the young men. They filled a booth inside as it was just too cold to sit outside. As they ate they rehashed the previous night's game as usual. The boys were in a good, but depressed mood, if such a thing is possible. They had played a tough team the night before and had come away victorious. They speculated on what would happen now that the team knew that Central Valley had beaten Lakota 21-20 the night before, ruining their chances for a league title. They all agreed there could be a big let down and that was something they had to avoid if they wanted to win back the 'bell'.

"We'll have to get 'em going in practice next week, JD," said Skipper.

"Yeah, I know, but I'm not sure we can."

"The seniors, Josh, Paul, and Bobby will help. You know they want to win this game!" said Gene, as he stuffed fries in his mouth.

"All I know is that we've got to win back that victory bell. After five years, it's about time we do it!" said Pete. "That's all my older brother talks about. He's always telling me that Fort Sage had the bell when he played!"

"I know, man!" said Skip. "Seems like that's all anyone is concerned with around this town. Five years! That's all we read in the paper, too. Man, we have got to win this game!"

Scott's usual brevity was evidenced again as all he said was, "It's doable. But it will be the toughest game we've played." Then he took a large bite out of his double hamburger.

The thought silenced the boys for a few moments until Ross, seemingly always happy, said, "Hey, we'll beat those bums. Now let's talk about some serious stuff, like who's got a date to the homecoming dance next Saturday. I know I'm going. Anybody else?"

As they went around the table, it was revealed that everyone had a date except JD. "Man, why don't you just ask the girl?" Skipper asked him, somewhat exasperated. "I'm going to text her right now!"

Embarrassed, JD just shrugged his shoulders. "Ah, I don't know. I doubt if she would go with me now. Besides, she probably already has a date."

"I don't think so," said Ross, "but Hector told me this morning that Maria told him that Stan had been after Wendy to go to the dance with him. If you want to go with her JD, you better get on the stick!"

JD nodded his head in agreement. He knew Ross was right. As his friends laughed and joked he finished his 1/2 pound burger in silence, his mind on the bell game and Wendy. He made up his mind to talk to her in the coming week.

The next four days sped by, and as his sixth period English class wound down on Thursday, JD found himself thinking more about trying to catch Wendy after school than about Shakespeare's Hamlet that they were studying. All week he had tried to catch a moment with her during lunch or after school. She had been surrounded by her girlfriends during lunch and he hadn't been able to find her after school. He didn't want to text her; he didn't think that would work. When the bell rang he quickly packed up his books, scribbled the assignment for that night in his notebook and headed out the door.

The weather was overcast and chilly so he buttoned up his letter jacket as he strode quickly down the walkway toward the end of the building. He glanced around the campus, searching the lockers at the end of the library for Wendy. As he made his way over toward her locker he saw her come around the corner with Maria. He stopped at the corner of the sidewalk to wait for her. He saw Wendy check her books, slam her locker shut and turn to walk to the gymnasium. After a couple of steps when Maria said goodbye and turned off to the right, JD thought he had the perfect chance to catch her alone.

Wendy glanced up and saw JD standing at the 'T' of the sidewalk. She smiled slightly, and waved. She felt herself becoming anxious, and she knew exactly why, hoping this would be the day he asked her to the dance.

JD returned her wave and moved to walk beside her.

"Hi Wendy, I wanted to ask you about..."

"Hey! Douglas! Douglas!" JD was interrupted by Coach Archer calling to him from his classroom door. He stopped and turned to see what was going on when Stan walked up on the other side of Wendy.

"JD? What did you..." Wendy started to ask.

"Hi Wendy! I'll walk you to the gym," JD heard Stan interrupt. He turned his back on Coach Archer.

"Hey Stan, just a minute, Wendy and I..." he began, but was interrupted again by the assistant coach calling his name.

"Douglas! Hey! Get over here! I want to show you something before practice!"

In a quandary, JD turned back to his coach. As he did Stan tugged on Wendy's elbow, leading her toward the gym.

"Hold on a second Stan," said Wendy, and as Stan tugged on her arm she gently pulled away.

"Just a minute coach!" JD called and then turned back to Wendy who was now two steps away, walking hesitantly by Stan, but looking over her shoulder at him.

"Wendy! Wait! Hey Stan! I said hold on!" Annoyed, JD was walking over to push Stan away when he felt Coach Archer's hand on his shoulder, pulling him toward the classroom. He glanced back over his shoulder at Wendy to see her still looking at him as Stan led her down the sidewalk.

"Wendy! Wait! I..." he called as his coach led him off.

He heard her call "bye" as he finally turned away to walk with his coach.

"Geez, coach! You sure have good timing!"

"What?" Coach Archer asked, "Something going on?"

"Forget it, Coach," said JD as he shook his head, smiling slightly in spite of what had happened. "What did you want to show me?" As they walked in the door he turned to glance one more time toward the gym, and saw Wendy and Stan engaged in conversation in front of the locker room.

"Can't anything go right?" he said to no one in particular.

Coach Archer, finally noticing what JD was talking about, grunted, and added, "Forget the girls, Douglas. We've got the bell game tomorrow!"

JD sighed, and playfully slapped his coach on the shoulder. "Coach, this better be good, because it may have cost me a date to the dance Saturday!"

"Douglas, you just worry about Friday night, and Saturday will take care of itself!"

"Coach, I sure hope you're right!"

Mac plopped himself down on his old office couch at 4:00AM Friday morning. He hadn't been able to sleep, so he had showered and come to school. It was only the Central Valley game that did this to him. Maybe it was because he wanted to beat them so badly. Maybe it was because he had grown up in Fort Sage, playing against them and all the while hating the Central Valley Spartans. Maybe it was because Central Valley bad mouthed every team they played, talked trash and played mind games. It was the one game of the year that still made him wish he could play again. It was kind of silly if one thought about it rationally, he told himself. But few ever thought about this game rationally.

'This is it,' he thought. 'Tonight is THE game. The whole town will be there. Probably be 6 thousand people in the stands and around the field. Maybe more tonight.'

The victory over Pine Bluff had upped their overall record to 4-3-1 and their league record to 3-1-1. They had already had a better year than any of the last four seasons. Still, Mac knew there were many in town who said his job depended on winning back that bell. Everyone knew that Fort Sage had played excellent football the last four games and they were playing at home. Even though there was no hope of a league title, the townspeople could sense the Wildcats had a real chance at beating Central Valley this year.

Mac rubbed his hands through his hair. Central Valley had twice the student body of Fort Sage. The Spartans were undefeated, and they had a bigger offensive and defensive line than his team, and they had speed. Only one or two of their players played both on offense and defense. Still, despite only having 6 seniors, it was true, his team did have an excellent chance this year. He mentally went through the week of practice in his mind. He had brought the team together every day in a meeting before practice to focus them on the game. He had told them everyday they were good enough to win, that they were playing better football than any team in the state right now. He had told them that nothing would ruin Central Valley's season more than Fort Sage beating them tonight. They would lose the bell, and Fort Sage would have the pleasure of spoiling their arch rival's undefeated season.

Monday they had watched films, and reviewed offense. Tuesday they had watched films, and reviewed defense. Wednesday he had let them practice that option series, even though he still didn't want to run it, and they had practiced special teams. Yesterday they had held a light practice, running through plays, and the team had reviewed video of Central Valley's offense one last time. Had they missed anything? He didn't think so. He leaned his head back on the arm rest, thinking he might catch a nap before classes started.

The thought that he had blown their chances at a league title by not playing Douglas in the River Bend game nagged endlessly at him. He wondered if he had been fair to the other players. It had bothered him ever since he had made the decision, and lost the game. But, as he reflected on the turn around Douglas had made, Mac felt inside he had done the right thing – for Douglas, but maybe not the rest of his players. It was unsettling. The first period bell rang all too soon.

CHAPTER 18

The team dressed out quietly that night. Even Ross, the prankster, was subdued. As Mac prowled around the locker room he wondered if they weren't a little too tight. Well, he thought, better to be too serious, than not serious enough. As they headed out for pregame warmups, Mac noticed the stands were already almost full. It was a cold, crisp, November night, although the wind was not blowing. A crescent moon was partially hidden by lazily drifting clouds. It was, what one would call, perfect fall football weather.

After the team returned to the locker room from their warmups Mac gathered them for his final talk. He always talked to them before each game, and he usually didn't try to get them too fired up, but tonight was different.

"Alright men," he began when they were settled. "Well, it's about time to get out there. Since this is our last game, I want to share some thoughts with you. A while back I asked you to win a game for me, and doggone it, you gave me the effort of your lives! This game tonight is yours." He looked at the 26 serious faces looking at him for a few seconds. "You have been as fine a group of men as I have ever worked with. We've been all over this - we know the papers say Central Valley is bigger, they say Central Valley has more seniors, they say Central Valley has speed. But, you know what? We coaches don't care! You juniors have played a whole season - you're senior football players for all practical purposes. We coaches know you are playing the best football in the state right now!"

He paused, then continued talking as he paced back and forth slowly. "I wanted to tell you tonight about the history of this game." His voice became more urgent. "Fort Sage has been playing Central Valley in football for over fifty years. In that time the overall record in the Bell Game is 34 to 19 in favor of Fort Sage! WE OWN THAT BELL!" Mac pounded his fist into his hand. "Over the years many fine men have played for Fort Sage in this game. They have sat in this very same locker room. Many will be in the stands tonight. Some of them are no longer with us on this earth, but believe this - living or dead, the spirit and the will of every single one of them will be on that field with you tonight. You'll be able to feel it! This is your night. We're not going to be intimidated anymore. WE ARE GOING TO WIN THIS GAME!"

"YEAH!!" yelled the players, some of them pumping their hands. Mac paused, his eyes burning, then in a loud voice said, "THIS GAME IS YOURS AND THAT BELL IS YOURS, NOW GO TAKE IT BACK!"

The Wildcats roared their agreement, shouting over and over "YES!" They jumped up to leave, the hearts pumping wildly with the adrenalin that flows before games. Mac caught Coach Archer's signal that it was time to take the field. On purpose, even if it meant missing the national anthem, Mac had told Coach Archer to wait until Central Valley had taken the field. Central Valley always tried to make the other team take the field first, but he had made up his mind to not play their games anymore. Caught up in the heat of moment he bolted for the door, slamming it open and ran out to the field leading his team down the sideline.

The home crowd roared and cheered as the Wildcats took the field, while the visiting Spartan fans booed. As the teams waited for the coin toss, JD took in the spectacle. Twenty-six Wildcats were lined up on the south sideline in their traditional home colors of royal blue jerseys, and gold pants. The Spartans, all 48 of them, stood on the north sideline in their blue pants, white jerseys with red numbers. Their white tops made them look even bigger than they were. Mac's pregame talk had caused JD to think about his father. I know he's watching tonight, JD thought to himself as he glanced around.

The entire Fort Sage football field was surrounded with people. Both the home and visiting stands were full. People were standing three deep outside the fence around the field. It was the biggest crowd he had ever played in front of. His warm breath was visible in the cold air. JD could feel the tension, like static electricity, in the air. Both teams were tight bows strings ready to be released.

He bounced up and down trying to stay warm and loose, searching the stands at the west 35 yard line for his mom and sister. He found them, and gave a short wave, then stopped and looked again. Who was that sitting by them? His attention was jerked back to the field by the epitaphs he could hear the Spartans shouting at the Fort Sage seniors as they went out for the final coin toss of the year. 'I hope I'm a captain next year,' he thought to himself.

The Wildcats won the toss and chose to defer their choice to the second half. Mac had wanted to go on defense first anyway. The kickoff team was the one special team JD didn't play on. He watched as the referee blew his whistle, and both stands stood and roared as Hector approached the ball, booting it down to the five yard line. To his horror he saw the speedy Central Valley deep back break two tackles and turn upfield down the visiting sidelines. The visiting fans roared and screamed as it appeared Central Valley would score on the opening kickoff. Only Skipper, running for all he was worth, prevented it with a touchdown saving tackle at the Fort Sage 40 yard line.

"Let's go defense!" shouted Mac as the referees blew their whistles and marked the ball. JD buttoned his chin strap on tight as he jogged on the field with the rest of the starting defensive team. From the beginning, the game was the hardest hitting affair of the year.

In the defensive huddle all of the Wildcats were telling each other it was time to stop them, right off, on this first series. The Spartans broke the huddle with a confident "break" and hurried to the line of scrimmage. They lined up in their most common offensive formation, split backs, with a split end to the left, tight end and flanker to the right. Their first play was a blast off the offensive right tackle. The Central Valley tight end double teamed Scott on the defensive left side and the flanker blocked down on Josh, the left side linebacker. The result was a giant hole off tackle through which burst the same speedy Central Valley back. He ripped off eight yards before JD, playing the monster slot dropped him with a crisp tackle. On second down,

Central Valley ran the same play to the right, this time gaining four yards, as Pete and JD made the tackle.

With a first down on the Wildcat 28 yard line, the Spartans were fired up. Their next play was a counter, out of the same offensive formation they had used the preceding two plays. This time, the determined Wildcats flew to the first fake to the right offensive side and when the counter back sped through the line against the grain he was able to break an arm tackle by Pete and Bobby, and break it outside down the home sidelines. Skipper ran him down on the five yard line, knocking him out of bounds. The Spartans now had first and goal on the four yard line!

"Let's go! Let's go!" shouted Josh, as the defense huddled.

"These guys are fast!" said a winded Skip.

"Come on line. Let's go!" Scott shouted, as Central Valley broke their huddle again.

Their next two running plays were stopped for no gain by the Wildcat 'gap 7' defense. On third down from the four, Central Valley tried a play action pass. The Spartan quarterback faked a dive to his fullback, then took a three step drop and fired a pass into the right corner of the endzone toward his crossing wide receiver. Skip was covering and he closed on the ball as it spiraled toward the receiver. He leaped in front of the receiver and swatted at the ball with his right hand. The football glanced off his hand and popped straight up into the air as both Skipper and the Spartan receiver fell to the turf. Skip landed on his face in the turf thinking he had broke up the play, but the football dropped straight down into the hands of the Spartan receiver that had fallen on his back in the corner of the endzone.

The sidejudge ran forward with both hands upraised. Central Valley had scored.

The Spartans converted the extra point despite a hard rush by Paul at the defensive end slot. As the visiting crowd cheered only the Wildcat players heard the taunts by the Spartan players as they jogged off the field pointing their fingers at the Wildcats.

Coach Roberts met Skipper at the sideline as the kickoff receiving team huddled.

"That's OK, Wilson. You made a good play, it was just bad luck. Now, let's get a good run back on this kickoff!"

The Central Valley kicker boomed the kick eight yards deep in the endzone, forcing the Wildcats to start from their own twenty yard line. JD huddled his team on the 20.

"Alright guys, let's get it back. Coach wants to run I formation, blast right. I formation, blast right. Ready - BREAK!"

The Wildcats ran up to the line, determined to gain back the touchdown. As JD called his signals, he watched the Central Valley defense shift right into the hole the play was supposed to run. Ross, the I-back, took the handoff on the blast, but only gained 3 yards before being thrown back. The visiting crowd roared. On second down Mac called for split backs, dive left. Again as he called his signals, JD watched the Spartans shift their strength into the very hole they were running. Pete was only able to pick up 3 yards, mostly on his own, bringing up 3rd and four on the Wildcat 26 yard line.

As the players unpiled the Spartans were again taunting the Wildcats. "You can't run on us, you losers! You might as well quit!"

Staying conservative deep in his own territory, Mac called another dive out of the double tight end formation, this time to the right. JD watched the Spartans shift again, but Pedro was able to break a tackle as he twisted when he hit the line of scrimmage and surge ahead for 5 yards giving the Wildcats a first down on the 31 yard line. For the first time the home crowd had something to cheer about, and they roared their approval.

"Boy, did we need that," Mac told Coach Archer on the headset. He sent his guard in with the play, a quick toss to the left, or home side of the field.

JD took the snap, and whirled to his left, tossing the ball to Ross as he broke out to the left. But Central Valley was playing a 6-2 defense, and their defensive end was on the outside of the Wildcat offensive line. He quickly came across and tackled Ross for a two yard loss. A second down blast did not gain an inch and the Wildcats faced a third and twelve.

Mac called for a screen to the right, or wide side of the field. JD took the snap and drifted back, looking deep down the left side of the field on purpose. Just before the onrushing defensive linemen closed in he passed the ball off to the right to Pete. He never saw what happened, as he was planted in the turf by two, large defensive lineman long after the pass was out of his hand.

Pete made the catch and turned upfield. He broke through one tackle at the thirty five, spinning around in a circle and making his way up the sideline. He was knocked hard out of bounds by a Central Valley player at the 43 yard line, and another Spartan laid a shoulder into his ribs as he skidded on the ground, clearly out of bounds.

Mac screamed for a late hit penalty, and the home crowd booed when no yellow flags were forthcoming. After the two first downs, the Wildcat offense stalled and gained only 5 yards on the next three plays. Each time JD noticed one or two Spartan defensive lineman would seem to shift to where the play was going. He was forced to punt the ball away as the first quarter ended.

The Spartans took over on their own 23 yard line to begin the second quarter and they continued right where they had left off on offense. Their large offensive line was double teaming the Fort Sage tackles and noseguard and their two fast backs were gaining four to eight yards with each run. The Wildcat secondary was making most of the tackles as the Spartans quickly marched down the field. Seven plays later found them at the Wildcat 22 yard line with a first down.

They tried a sweep to the short side of the field and picked up 8 yards before JD and Bobby knocked the ball carrier out of bounds with a crushing tackle on his left hip. As they jumped up to return to the huddle, the Central Valley back limped toward his bench grabbing the top of his hip.

On second down from the 14, the Spartan quarterback dropped back to attempt only his third pass of the game. The Wildcat secondary maintained good coverage, forcing him to hold the ball too long. Scott, using a 'swim' move, forced aside the back blocking him and bore down on the Spartan quarterback, smashing him hard into the turf for a loss of seven yards. The home crowd roared.

"Alright defense! Way to stick Scott!" shouted Coach Roberts and the entire Wildcat sideline.

On third down the Spartans tried the counter that had gained them big yards when they scored in the first quarter. The Central Valley back was able to gain 15 yards down to the Wildcat six yard line, but the Spartans were called for holding on the play. The ball was brought back to the Wildcat 31 yard line after the ten yard penalty, causing the visiting fans to boo loudly. Facing third and 19, Central Valley tried another pass that was knocked down by JD in a vicious collision with the Spartan receiver that had the entire visiting crowd screaming for pass interference.

On fourth down, the Spartans brought out their long kicker and converted a 48 yard field goal! Fearing a fake because of the great distance, the Wildcats had only rushed 7 men and did not put much pressure on the kicker. Still, they had stopped the touchdown drive and as the defense jogged off the field, the home crowd cheered their effort.

As JD and Skip lined up for the kickoff, down 10-0 halfway through the second quarter, they knew the team had to get it going.

"Come on JD. We've got to run this one back far!"

"I know it. We need some points bad."

JD had already made up his mind that he was going to run the kick back no matter what. The Central Valley kicker booted the ball to the Fort Sage one yard line, where JD caught it and yelled to Skipper to "Come on!" The two broke to the home side of the field where the return was set up. As he crossed the ten yard line right behind Skipper, JD could see the picket line collapsing.

"Break it right!" he shouted as he cut back. Hearing him, Skipper swerved and took out one potential tackler with a hard block square on his chest. That gave

JD a little room and he kicked it in to high gear trying to turn the right corner on the return team. He could see he had two men to beat. A white jerseyed tackler grabbed his shoulder as JD flew by him, causing him to twist in a circle. JD planted his right foot and cut sharply back to the left to leave another Central Valley player grabbing air, and the corner was his. He turned up the visiting sideline, swiftly eating up yards, passing the 20, 30 and 40 yard lines. JD could see the Spartan kickoff team safety angling over to cut him off and he knew he couldn't outrun the angle the defensive man had on him.

As he crossed midfield and just before the Spartan closed on him he purposely cut back into him. The Central Valley player skidded as he reacted to JD's cut. When JD ran past he reached out and was able to grab his jersey with both hands. JD surged powerfully forward and twisted in a circle trying to break the Spartan's hold. The Central Valley player was dragged three yards before he finally lost his hold and fell to the ground.

JD had been slowed down considerably and the release of the extra weight caused him to stumble forward. As he reached out with his left hand to push off the ground and regain his balance, two Central Valley players plowed hard into his back, driving him down to the field at the Central Valley 41 yard line.

As he lay on the ground a third Spartan speared him in the back with his helmet, driving the football into his diaphragm and forcing all of the air out of him. He rolled over, groaning and trying to suck air into his lungs unsuccessfully.

Seeing the spear by the Central Valley player the

home crowd went wild, screaming for a penalty. At the same instant a yellow flag was thrown by the head referee, landing right next to where JD lay.

As the referees were marking off the penalty, JD slowly rolled over, still not able to take a full breath, and got up. He weakly made his way back to his huddle, his back aching. He could hear the Central Valley bench yelling at him, telling him there was more where that came from. But, the penalty had cost the Spartans. It moved the football down to the Central Valley 26 yard line, where the Wildcats had a first down.

Fired up by the return, the team loudly broke the huddle as they came to the line to run the dive Mac had called. As JD called his signals the Spartans shifted their defense and the play went for no gain. A second down sweep gained 4 yards, bringing up a third and 6 at the 22 yard line. The clock was down to four minutes and running. JD used one of the Wildcats three time-outs and jogged over to talk to Mac and Coach Roberts.

"Why'd you call timeout John? You feeling OK?" Coach Roberts asked. He had seen the hit JD had taken.

"I'm alright coach. It's a little hard to breath, though."

JD waited as Mac talked to Coach Archer on the headset for a few seconds. His stomach hurt and his back was already tightening up. When Mac was done, he started to tell JD the play to run. JD interrupted.

"Coach, may I say something?"

Surprised, Mac nodded.

"I called timeout to tell you every time we run our dives, sweeps, or blasts they shift their defense right where we want to run. That's why our plays don't work."

Mac considered this. He usually didn't make

decisions based on what his players said, but Coach Archer had also mentioned the shifting defense earlier.

John spoke again, "Coach, they must have scouted our formations, and I think they're guessing what we'll run off each one."

"Humph," Mac grunted. He knew his time was running out. He hurried, "Alright, we've got third and six. Get in there and run I formation, double tight ends."

"Coach!" interrupted JD "They'll just shift..."

"Quiet! Let me finish Douglas! Run double tight ends, flanker right, counter back off the dive right to Ross on the left side! Almost everything we do from now on is misdirection or pass – out of formations that are the opposite of what we have used."

JD smiled as he recognized his mistake in jumping to conclusions with his coach. "Sure thing coach! It'll work!"

"Get going, the ref's blowing the whistle! Hurry! No delay penalty!"

JD ran back to the huddle and called the play, hurrying the offense up to the line. As he called his signals he watched the Central Valley defense shift over to the offensive right side. 'This aughta go,' he thought. He was right, as Ross ripped off 12 yards on the counter play. It was the first big run Fort Sage had all night from the line of scrimmage.

The ball was now on the 10 yard line, first down and goal. Mac called for a bootleg to the short side of the field. JD watched as the Spartans again shifted to cover the right side as he barked out his signals. He took the snap, faked the handoff on the sweep to the right, then tucked the ball on his hip as he bootlegged out to the left and headed for the endzone corner. Only the short sideline prevented him from scoring as almost the entire Central Valley defense was out of position. He was forced out of bounds by the Spartan cornerback on at the three yard line, then hit late in the back again by the Spartan safety after he was out of bounds. The resulting penalty put the ball on the one and a half yard line, with a first down!

Craftily, Mac purposely called a straight dive on first down to set up a play action pass on second down. Pete, bulling ahead on his powerful legs, almost scored on the dive. On second down, JD faked the same dive, then pulled the ball out and laid a soft pass to the Paul, the tight-end, wide open in the middle of the endzone. The home stands erupted in a loud continuous roar. Fort Sage had scored!

Unfortunately, Josh's snap on the extra point was in the grass and bounced to JD. By the time the ball was set the onrushing Central Valley line blocked the kick. With less than two minutes to go in the half the score stood 10-6 in favor of Central Valley.

The fired up Wildcat defense was able to keep it right there as they shut down the Spartan offense after the kickoff, and the half ended with Fort Sage down by four points.

As Mac followed the team to the locker room, he was cautiously optimistic. They seemed to have found something there, toward the end of the half.

In the locker room JD went over with Mac and Coach Archer what he had noticed about Central Valley's shifting of players on defense. He wanted badly to suggest the use of the option series, but didn't. Mac indicated they were going to stick with the misdirection plays out of formations they hadn't usually ran the plays from. Coach Roberts talked with Robert and Scott about the double teaming they were facing all first half. The coaches decided to move the defensive tackles out on the outside shoulder of the offensive tackle instead of 'headup'. They hoped this would reduce the offensive tackle's ability to double team and maybe confuse them. All of the players mentioned the taunting by the Central Valley players, it was starting to get under their skin.

The 15 minute break passed all too quickly and Mac gathered his team before he sent them out one last time.

"Men, you've got two quarters of football left this season. You make the most of them. Don't leave anything in reserve. This is it. We think we've got these guys figured out! You are playing a fine ballgame, keep it up. Don't let their big mouths get to you. That's what they want. We'll let the score do our talking. Remember what I told you earlier. We own that bell! We've got two quarters left to take it back! Now let's get after it! We're going to win this thing!"

Mac's short talk had shaken the natural lethargy that sets in at halftime from the players. They headed out to the field quieter than at the beginning of the game, but just as determined. Mac knew his team would receive the second half kickoff. If they could take it down and score, they just might get this team on the run.

Skipper received the second half kickoff at the goal line and was able to return out to the 32 yard line before he was brought down hard by several white jerseyed players. The hitting, if anything, was harder in the second half of the game than the first. At times it seemed like shotguns were going off on the field as the pads and helmets of the players popped together.

Mac opened up the offense in the third quarter, calling several counters, misdirections and pass plays. JD connected three times with Skip on crossing patterns and the Wildcats sharply moved the ball against a Spartan defense that was now back on its heels a little. The offense moved the ball from its own 32 down to the Central Valley 19 yard line. It looked to everyone as if Fort Sage was ready to score a go ahead touchdown.

They faced a second down 5 and Mac called a pass play that had Skipper lined up at flanker on the left side. He was to break straight up field ten yards, out to the sideline and then upfield again. The split end on the left also broke straight upfield ten yards, then in across the middle. The tight end on the right side did an up an out pattern. Against the 3 deep zone played by Central Valley, Mac was hoping Wilson would be open down the sideline.

JD called his signals on the line, noting how the Spartans had quit shifting their players around. He took the snap and dropped back, purposely looking at his tight end on the right side of the field. After a count of two he looked for Skipper and saw that he was blanketed. His crossing wide receiver was covered also. His offensive line protection broke down and he was about to be sacked for a loss when he tried to dump a short pass out in the flat to Ross who had released as a safety valve. His arm was hit by an onrushing defensive end just as he released the ball and it floated high over Ross's head.

The last thing he saw as he was slammed down on his back was the Central Valley linebacker that was covering Ross on the play jump and snatch the football out of the air on the run at the 27 yard line and head straight down the home sideline with Ross gamely trying to reverse his direction and give chase. The Spartan won the footrace with his running head start and carried the ball in for the touchdown as the visiting fans went nuts in the stands.

Central Valley converted the extra point and the score, and instead of the score being 13-10 in favor of Fort Sage toward the end of the third quarter, now ominously, it was 17-6 in favor of Central Valley!

It had been a huge mistake! One JD knew he shouldn't have made. He should have taken the sack. How many times had Mac told the quarterbacks not to try to do too much? Despite Mac telling him it was 'OK' as he jogged in for the kickoff receiving huddle, JD knew Mac was not happy and that Fort Sage was really up against it now. That drive had used up nine minutes and they hadn't gotten anything for it. He felt terrible.

The Spartan kicker put the kickoff out of the endzone, prohibiting any runback and forcing the Wildcats to start at their own 20 yard line, down by 11 with a little over two minutes left in the third quarter. Things didn't look good. Mac tried to settle things down by calling running plays. He didn't want to risk another turnover right now. Central Valley, however, was now playing everything the Wildcats did 'headup' and they had quit shifting their defensive linemen. The Wildcats weren't gaining yardage like they were on that first drive of the third quarter. The Spartan coaches had adjusted to Fort Sage's offensive changes.

They gained one first down, then bogged down at the 35 yard line after a holding penalty. Facing a third and 13 Mac tried another pass, but the Spartan coaches expected just this and brought eight men after

JD. He thought for an instant he had a chance to connect with Skip down the middle, but the risk of interception weighed on him, causing him to hesitate. He was smashed down brutally hard by three defensive linemen.

JD got up slowly again; he knew they would have to give the ball up. His chin had been split open on the last hit and it was bleeding down onto his jersey as he lined up to punt the ball away. He took the long snap from Josh and launched a high, wobbly spiral down to the Central Valley 12 yard line where it bounced out of bounds.

As the Wildcat defense huddled over the ball, everyone knew they needed the football back fast. For the first time in the second half the Spartan offense took the field. Trying to burn time off the clock, they stuck with their same running plays of the first half. The adjustments made by Coach Roberts caused confusion in the offensive line and the steady Wildcat defense was able to hold them to a gain of only six yards in three plays. On fourth down, the Wildcats went for the block, rushing 10 men with only JD back to return the kick. Paul nearly blocked the kick from the left side with a hard rush that culminated in him leaping high over the offensive back assigned to block him. But the kick barely sailed by his outstretched fingers.

JD caught the kick at the Wildcat 40 yard line but was only able to return it back to midfield before he was swarmed by the Spartans as the horn went off signaling the end of the third quarter.

The visiting fans and team all at once put their hands in the air with four fingers held up, yelling out a long, drawn out, "FOUUUUUUR!" to show that 'they controlled the fourth quarter'. As one, the Wildcat fans stood and booed, pointing fingers at the Spartan side of the field.

Every team that played Central Valley hated it when they did this, and Mac especially disliked it. He called his entire team together for a huddle at midfield while the Spartan fans and players held up their hands and yelled.

"Alright boys, this is our last quarter. We're going to win this thing!" he yelled. "Everybody get in here – get in here! WHAT ARE WE?" he asked loudly.

"Wildcats!" the team shouted rather weakly.

"I CAN'T HEAR YOU!" Mac yelled. "WHAT ARE WE?"

"WILDCATS! WILDCATS!" shouted the players.

"Alright! Let's go! We're going to score right now!" Then he broke the huddle as the referees marked the ball ready for play and the Spartans quit their yelling. Before he ran on the field, JD went up to Mac.

"Coach, let's try that option series. They'll won't be able to handle it."

"Douglas, just get on the field and run the play!" Mac said impatiently. He didn't want to hear about any fool option series, especially with this game on the line.

"Coach," JD pleaded, "let's try it. We're down 11 points. I don't think we have time for two long drives!"

Coach Roberts had heard what JD was saying and as the refs blew their whistles signaling the ball ready for play, he quickly jumped in. "He's right, Mac. Time's short. Let's try it."

"Not Now!" said Mac impatiently. "Douglas, get out there and run that counter. Hurry up!"

JD ran to the huddle to call the play.

"What you an' coach talking about, JD?" asked Skipper.

"No time now. I want to run the option. Coach said no. Alright, let's go. I-formation, counter left to Ross. On two. On two. Ready, break!"

JD called his signals and ran the play. Ross gained six yards, bringing up a second and four. Mac called a post pattern pass to Skip. JD took the snap, dropped back and sailed the ball right at Skipper's numbers, and he thought he had thrown a touchdown pass. The home fans groaned loudly as it was knocked down by a diving Central Valley safety at the last instant. Fortunately, a third down sweep with Pete gained five yards and a first down.

On first down, at the Spartan 39 yard line, Mac called for the same counter, only to Pete this time. The powerful fullback took the handoff from JD, busted through the line and the attempted tackle of the Central Valley linebacker and into the secondary. He gained 12 yards before he was tackled by the Spartan safety. Now Fort Sage had the ball at the 27 yard line!

An off tackle dive with Pete gained four yards. Ross took a quick pitch left for four more. On third down and two Pete busted right up the middle for 3 yards and a first down at the 16 yard line! The home fans cheered loudly as the chains were moved, the only trouble was the clock was moving to. It was now down to only 8 minutes left in the game!

Mac ran a guard in calling for a bootleg left again. JD thought for a minute, then said, "Skipper, line up on the right and head for the left endzone corner. I might throw this to you."

"What's that? That's not in this play! I'm supposed to break outside right!" he questioned.

"I know it!" snapped JD, "No time to argue. I've got a hunch you'll be wide open."

Suddenly realizing the potential of the adjustment Skip smiled broadly. "Roger that! I'll be there!"

"Alright you guys, let's get a good fake on this bootleg. You offensive linemen make sure you don't go downfield. We're going to score! Bootleg left, bootleg left! On two, on two! Ready, BREAK!"

JD brought the fired up team to the line of scrimmage, called his signals, and took the snap on the second "Hut". He faked the sweep to Ross going right, then tucked the ball on his hip as he circled to his left, trying to turn the corner for the score. The Central Valley defensive end that had been burned earlier recognized the play and closed quickly on JD, joined by the Spartan cornerback on the right defensive side.

JD made a deep curve back to the 20 yard line to avoid the defensive end that was able to get a hand on his jersey before he slipped off and fell to the grass. As both stands squealed in excitement, JD looked up to see the oncoming corner. He knew he couldn't make it to the goal-line! Then, out of the corner of his eye he saw a royal blue jersey streaking across the endzone, wide open. He stopped, squared his shoulders and fired his pass right on target, leading Skipper by two steps.

The onrushing corner plowed right into him as he released the ball, hitting him straight in the chin with his helmet. The blow knocked JD flat on his back, causing him to see stars. The coagulated cut on his chin began to bleed again. As he fell down, the roar of the home stands told JD what he could not see. Skip had scored a touchdown! The Wildcat players were jumping with excitement, slapping each other on the back!

JD rolled over and groggily got to his feet. Mac called for a timeout to review two point conversion options. The score was now 17-12, Central Valley. He knew one point wasn't going to do Fort Sage any good and if they made the two point try they would be able to tie with a field goal.

JD sluggishly approached coach Mac and Coach Roberts on the sideline; it was apparent he was really beginning to feel the beating he had taken during the game. His ribs, bruised in the Pine Bluff game, had been hit again; his back was aching and his bleeding chin had stained his jersey front with dark blotches.

"You alright, John?" asked Mac, calling him by his first name, something he had rarely done all season. JD took in a deep, painful breath, grimacing slightly.

"I'm OK coach, just a little sore in the ribs."

"Yeah, I'll bet!" said Mac admiringly. He knew the game had been a severely hard hitting contest, and he had seen the hits JD had taken. "Hey, what the heck was Wilson doing running a cross on that bootleg anyway? We've never practiced that."

JD was briefly afraid Mac was angry. He looked him the eye and said, "I just had a hunch coach. Their secondary has been flying to the ball on runs."

"Hummph!" Mac grunted. He had never liked his teams doing anything other than he had called, but it had worked. "Good thinking," he said grudgingly. "Grab yourself a drink!" He handed JD a squirt bottle. He was beginning to see, for the first time, JD's ability to think on the field. Why hadn't he noticed that earlier in the year?

Mac turned to his assistant, Keith, standing next to him. "Well, Coach, what you think for the two point conversion? We don't have much time."

"George says we ought to run that option pass we used against Lakota. I think it'll work."

"I don't know. These guys have scouted us pretty well. They'll probably be looking for that."

"How about blasting Pete up the middle?" offered Coach Roberts.

Mac sighed. This was what being the head coach came down to. You had to make your choices and hope they worked. No one else would make them for you. It was sometimes gut-wrenching. He thought for a few seconds as he looked at his play chart. "I don't think that'll work, coach. Our boys have been going both ways all night. Their defensive line is bigger and fresher. I think we'll try play action to Ross on a dive to the left, then dump the ball off to Silva in the right flat. He is strong enough to punch that thing in if he's close."

He looked at JD standing in front of him. "Got that Douglas?" When JD nodded he continued. "Alright, get out there. Pro set, play action left, ends run off the corners, quick screen right to Silva. Got it?"

"Got it coach!" said a fresher JD. Then he turned and ran back to the huddle.

JD explained the play in detail in the huddle then brought the team to the line. Both stands were roaring as he called signals. They realized the importance of the play. JD took the snap on the third "Hut!" and whirled to his left, faking a handoff to Ross on a dive. He quickly took three steps back, purposely looking toward the left endzone corner. Then, as the pocket began to collapse, he spiraled the football out to Pete in the right flat at the five yard line. He watched the rest of the play unfold in front of him, unable to help.

Pete had made a looping run out to the side and he

gathered the ball in on the run toward the goal line. The crowd roar became even louder as he tucked the ball away in his right hand and lowered his shoulders, aiming for the goal line.

A Spartan linebacker and cornerback were angling in on him to make the tackle, with the defensive safety bringing up the rear. The Wildcat right tackle, Scott, had headed straight down the line of scrimmage after releasing his block on the Spartan defensive tackle. His block cut down the Central Valley linebacker. Pete, seeing the other two Spartan players coming, tried to deliver a blow with his left forearm as they hit him at the two yard line. The ensuing 'crack' sounded almost like a lightning strike, and caused the crowd to let out a loud "ooohhh!"

The force of the collision sent the Central Valley corner flying back on his back, but the safety wrapped Pete up around the shoulders. Pete's strength in his legs allowed him to surge forward to the one, dragging the white jerseyed defensiveman with him. As he fell across the goal line, the other Central Valley defensive safety drove his shoulder hard into Pete's chest, his helmet striking the football Pete carried in his right arm, sending it flying up in the air and backwards.

The next events all occurred almost simultaneously. The backjudge rushed forward from the back of the endzone, raising his hands to signal the two point try good! The football bounced crazily out of bounds at the three yard line! The referee on that side of the field ran forward crossing his arms in front of him to signal the try no good!

Neither the fans, nor either team knew if it had been good or not. The resulting confusion lasted nearly three minutes as the referees huddled to discuss whether or not Pete had possession of the ball as he crossed the goal line. Both the home and visiting fans were yelling and offering their opinions. Mac, standing on the home sidelines at the 35 yard line, felt helpless. The Wildcat offense and Spartan defense both waited on the field as the officials talked excitedly with each other.

Finally, the wait ended, and the white capped, head referee emerged from the circle of stripped shirts to signal the try NO GOOD! The home stands erupted in a chorus of boos, drowned out by the screams of joy from the visiting fans. JD felt his heart sink. Now the Wildcats had to have nothing less than a touchdown and less than seven minutes remained on the clock!

As the offense jogged off the field, Pete hung his head low. JD knew how he felt, having thrown that interception earlier. He crossed over to him and put his arm on Pete's shoulder pads.

"It's OK, Pete, you made a heck of a run. We'll get it back!"

Pedro looked up at him with agonized eyes. "I blew it. Should've held onto the ball. Man, I just blew it!" He slapped his helmet hard against his right thigh pad as they reached the sidelines and glumly walked to the water table for a drink.

Central Valley ran Fort Sage's kickoff back to their own 29 yard line, where their offense took over. The Spartan coach knew time was on his side as long as he team didn't have a turnover. With three or four first downs the game was his.

The Wildcat defense was just acutely aware of the situation. Despite being disappointed with the failed two point try, they exhorted each other to "Fire up!"

and get the ball back. Tired though they were from having to play both ways all night, they were still a grim and determined group of young men.

Central Valley, adjusting their play calling to Fort Sage's change in their defensive tackle alignment, began to gain yardage up the middle. In three plays they gained 13 yards and a first down, burning the clock down to 5 and half minutes. After getting the news from Coach Archer in the booth, Coach Roberts began to call tackle 'pinches' on the next series of downs. Two plays later the Spartans faced a third and five on their own thirty-seven yard line.

As they broke their huddle, the home stands let a long, drawn out "aaaaaaaaaah!" while the quarterback barked his signals. On defense, JD didn't expect a pass, thinking that the Central Valley coach wouldn't risk it. He began to cheat closer to the line from his monster slot on the strong side. To his surprise the ball was snapped and the quarterback dropped backwards to pass!

He quickly dropped back into coverage and saw the offensive flanker on his side break out to the sideline as the tight end headed straight up field and out. JD had to take the tight end in coverage and Bobby had the flanker. The Spartan quarterback, hurried by Paul rushing from the left, still laid the ball almost perfectly in front of his flanker on the sideline. It looked like a sure first down completion, until Bobby flew in from behind the receiver, driving hard at his outside shoulder. The ball, Bobby and the receiver all met at the same instant, and the ball bounced high off the receiver's pads out of bounds!

The Spartan coaches and fans screamed for a pass

interference call, but there wasn't any penalty called! The home fans roared their approval. It was now fourth and five!

The Central Valley coach decided not to risk going for the first down and the Spartans lined up to punt the ball away. Again, JD was the only deep back, with the other ten defensive players rushing the punter. Unfortunately, the offensive blocking was strong and the punter booted the ball downfield, purposely out of bounds to keep it out of JD's hands. With five minutes left in the game the Wildcats took over on their own 25 yard line needing a touchdown to win the game!

Figuring the Spartans would be looking for passes Mac stuck with running plays the first two calls. The first down counter to Pete gained only four yards, and on second down the Wildcats managed only three yards on a sweep to the home side of the field. Facing third and three, Mac called his second timeout of the half and motioned for JD to come over to talk. They met at the hashmark on the 40 yard line.

Determined to speak first, JD swallowed hard, then began. He was prepared to argue now if he had to. "Coach, we've got to run that option series to loosen these guys up. They'll never expect it!"

"NO, we don't want a fumble now!"

"Coach, now is the time! It'll work! Just let us try it! We've got to do something new! There's only 4 minutes left in the game and we've got to go almost seventy yards to score! Let's try it!" JD spoke urgently, but not disrespectfully.

Mac's first inclination was to tell JD to keep quiet, he was running the team and if JD didn't be quiet, he was going to go sit on the bench! In fact the words were halfway out of his mouth, when he stopped himself. Douglas's ability to think on the field had already been demonstrated, especially by the change in the bootleg he made with Wilson for the TD. For a full 10 seconds he mulled it over.

"Alright. Maybe you're right Douglas. OK, get in there and go over it with the team. We can't afford a turnover, though. No fumbles! Let's run the read option to the right on this play. If we don't get a first down, call the roll out - post, flag, out pass. Got it?"

JD smiled. He was excited. "Got it! Don't worry, coach. We'll get the first!" Then he turned and ran back to the huddle to go over the play.

At the line, JD looked over the defense, barked his signals and took the snap. He turned to his right and rode the football in Pete's stomach as he looked at the line of scrimmage. Seeing there wasn't any running room, he pulled it out and continued down the line, looking at the defensive end with Ross trailing him for a pitch.

The Spartan defensive end didn't know what to do, seeing both JD running at him and Ross waiting for a pitch. He decided to tackle JD. When he committed to that, JD deftly flicked the ball out to Ross who turned the corner. The Central Valley defense was caught unawares and Ross ripped off 18 yards before he was knocked out of bounds at the fifty yard line! The play had worked perfectly! On the sidelines, Mac said softly to himself, "Well, I'll be...."

JD hurried over to get a play from Mac on the sidelines.

"Keep it going, Douglas! Run it again!" yelled a thoroughly surprised Mac.

The Wildcats ran the same play. This time the Spartan defensive end ran toward Ross to prevent the pitch, and when he did JD tucked the ball in his arm and turned straight upfield. He broke through the arm grab by the Central Valley linebacker and cut out toward the sidelines, picking up another 16 yards before he was tackled by the Spartan safety. The home fans were roaring and cheering nonstop now, as the clock ran down under three minutes.

From the sidelines, Mac motioned to JD to keep running the option series. JD called it to the left, this time handing off to Pete up the middle for seven yards, putting the ball on the Spartan 27 yard line! The Spartan coach called time out to try and make some adjustments. On the Wildcat sideline, Mac and Coach Roberts told JD to keep it going until Central Valley stopped it.

On second down from the 27 yard line, the 'Cats ran the option to the right side. JD faked to Pete up the middle and turned the ball upfield when the defensive end took Ross. He was hit hard by the linebacker almost immediately and gained only four yards, but enough for a first down.

With the clock running down to two minutes, JD got Mac's signal and ran the option to the left. Seeing no room for Pete up the middle he pulled the ball out and headed down the line. The defensive end was coming down hard on him, so he flicked the ball out to Ross. But Central Valley hadn't gone undefeated by accident. They were a good team and their adjustments were starting to pay off. The defensive corner tackled Ross for no gain and the visiting stands erupted! Trying to save their last timeout, JD quickly huddled the team and ran the option to the right again, handing off to Pete who was able to gain seven yards down to the 16 yard line!

Facing third and three, a running clock, and sensing the option was bogging down, Mac ran a guard in with a pass play. JD faked to Pete on the right side on a play action dive then he dropped quickly back, squared his shoulders and fired a pass to Skipper breaking across the middle from left to right. Skipper gathered it in and held on despite being sandwiched between two defenders in a loud, crackling tackle!

The home fans were going nuts! The Wildcats had first and goal at the eight yard line! Still trying to save their only remaining timeout, JD quickly huddled the offense at the eight yard line, waiting for the play from the sidelines. Mac ran a guard in with another pass play. JD quickly hurried the team to the line.

At the snap he dropped back fast, checking side to side for a receiver. With the field now shortened by the endzone, the advantage belonged to the defensive secondary and JD couldn't find anyone open. To avoid a sack, he threw the ball out of the endzone, stopping the clock with 1:34 remaining.

As he turned to get in the huddle, he heard the referee asking for the 'white' captain. 'Oh No! Not a penalty now,' he thought. But there was a penalty, on the Wildcats! The call was offensive holding, and it carried a 10 yard penalty with it!

As the referee marched off the penalty the visiting fans cheered raucously, and the home crowd booed. On the sideline Mac was furious. "Why didn't I run the option again?" he angrily asked himself. He forced himself to stay calm and consider the next play. He now faced first and goal from the 18 yard line, not the eight. He decided to run the option to the right side, telling the guard carrying the play in to tell JD and Ross to get out of bounds, if they could, at the end of the play.

On the field, JD gathered his teammates and tried to calm them.

"Alright, guys, we've got plenty of time. Don't worry. Coach wants option right, option right - ready? BREAK!" At the snap JD whirled right and rode Pete in the stomach with the ball as he eyed the line of scrimmage. He saw an opening up the middle and released the ball into Pete's grasp. Pete hit the line with full power, slamming into the back of Scott, his right tackle. The pile of bodies slowly surged forward as Pete took the ball down to the 12 yard line! The Wildcats now faced a second and goal from the 12 yard line with a running clock.

The clock was ticking down under a minute when JD took the snap for the second down call, option series left. He faked the dive up the middle to Pete, then faked a pitch to Ross and turned the ball upfield. He was hit in the left hip just as he passed the line of scrimmage. JD struggled through that tackle, twisting and pumping his legs, dragging another defensive man with him. The home crowd roared as he gained yardage up field. He was brought down by the safety and cornerback after picking up 6 more yards!

J.D.'s run had moved the ball down to the 6 yard line but the clock continued to run! Thirty eight seconds were showing on the scoreboard clock when the Wildcats broke their huddle for their third down play. Mac had ran a guard in with the directions to stay with the option, and hand off to Pete up the middle if possible.

At the snap JD turned to his left, eyed the defensive tackle and handed off to Pete, as his coach had asked. The Central Valley defensive team flew to the line of scrimmage causing a huge pile up. Pete was only able to gain 3 yards and move the ball down to the three. Facing fourth down and goal from the three, JD called the Wildcat's last time out with 14 seconds left in the game!

He jogged over to the sidelines to confer with Coach Roberts and Coach Mac. On the home sidelines, Mac and Coach Roberts were already hurriedly discussing the teams fourth down play when JD ran up, taking off his helmet. The Spartan coach had his entire defense huddled with him on the left hashmark. Mac looked over his play sheet, quietly considering his options on pass plays. He knew they had to go into the endzone and he didn't think his tired offensive team could push it in on the ground. It was 'crunch' time and JD, Coach Roberts and Mac all knew it. It was not a place for the fainthearted.

After a quick drink, JD looked up at his coach, waiting.

Mac let out a long sigh. He wasn't really sure what to run, but he was leaning toward some type of pass. After consulting with Coach Archer on the headset, he decided.

"We're going to run I formation, split left. I want play action to Pete up the middle. Have Wilson and the flanker drag across the endzone, crossing with the tight end. Ross releases to the flat. Got it?"

He nodded his head. "Got it, coach."

"Alright," he slapped JD on the shoulder pads, "Get out there and get it going. This is it. Remember, anything short of the goal-line doesn't do us any good at all. You can do it!" Then he pushed JD toward the huddle.

Back in the huddle, JD called the play, repeating it three times. He looked at his battle weary teammates, covered with sweat and dirt. Eight of them had played both ways all night against a Central Valley team that had used only two players both ways. This group had given everything they had and then some. But as he looked into each one's eyes, he knew that they were ready to give it all one last time. He had the sudden thought that win or lose he would never forget their faces as he saw them now.

"Alright guys, this is for the all the marbles. Everybody ready?"

As one, they answered, in low, grim voices, "Ready!"

He called for the break and hustled them up to the line.

Both the home and visiting fans began a long unending chant of "AHHHHHHHHHH" as the teams lined up.

On the line, JD looked at the eyes of the Central Valley players. He could tell they all meant business. Years later he would remember the next few moments as if they occurred in slow motion.

The nonstop yelling of the crowd was tuned out as he carefully wiped his hands on the towel hanging on the center's belt, and fitted his mouthpiece on his teeth. Next, he carefully hunched over center and placed his hands to take the snap, eyeing the defense. He called his signals, yelling them out as loud as he could, "READY BLUE!! READY BLUE!! SET!! HUT!

HUT!" Josh slammed the football into his hands. JD took the snap, and whirled to the right, riding the ball in Pete's stomach. The playside linebacker had to respect the fake and closed on the line to make the hit. JD pulled the ball out and dropped back fast, looking for an open receiver. He could see Skipper crossing from the left, deep in the endzone, not yet open. His tight end and flanker crossed in a semi-pick play, but the defensive secondary stayed right with them.

Ross chopped the onrushing defensive left end, then released out to the left flat as JD moved in the pocket, checking the endzone. The defensive left end rolled and was on his feet catlike, lunging toward JD. JD could feel, not see, the end coming. Also, the linebacker that had stepped up to tackle Pete on the fake had just kept coming, giving the defensive team a rush of eight men against the six Fort Sage blockers. Both the linebacker and the defensive end had broken through and were bearing down on the Wildcat quarterback. He was out of time!

He never heard the screams of the crowd as he instinctively, tucked the ball in his right arm and ducked, causing the onrushing defensive end to fly over his back. He broke out of the pocket to his right. He turned and stiff armed the diving left defensive end, and gave ground deep into the backfield to get around the corner and headed toward the corner of the goal line. The offensive and defensive players on the field were mixed in a mess of ordered confusion as JD gamely tried to avoid being tackled.

Scott, the right side offensive tackle, peeled back and leveled two defenders chasing him with a tremendous blind side block. JD was hit hard on the hip by the other Central Valley linebacker, and he spun with the force of the blow, broke free and clawed his way toward the four yard line. A defensive lineman grabbed at his left shoulder but couldn't wrap his arms and JD sidestepped quickly toward the right. A diving Spartan grabbed at his left leg causing JD to stumble forward, putting his left hand out to prevent his knee from touching.

The crowd was in total bedlam, as he regained his balance and cut sharply toward the sideline, heading for the goal line corner with a burst of speed. A glance toward Skipper showed he might have a chance to get him the ball on a pass, but he could see the safety shadowing his receiver closely, and he knew it wasn't a sure thing. He decided to run himself! There was no chance to break back left as there were too many defenders trailing him already. It was a foot-race now, and the left defensive corner that was coming up hard had the angle.

When he crossed the four, the clock was ticking off the final 3 seconds. He took two more strides and lowered his shoulder, preparing for the hit he knew he would take from the defensive players that seemed all at once to surround him.

Just before impact, a blue blur flashed across his field of vision, smashing into the Central Valley corner with a horrendous crunch. Skipper had peeled back to block when he saw JD make the decision to run. At the two yard line JD planted his right foot and leaped forward with all his strength. At the same time he felt a blow in the back from the helmet of one of the trailing Spartans, and a smash in the left shoulder from the Central Valley safety.

He landed with his entire upper body across the line. The hit from the pursuing defenders had actually propelled him further into the endzone! He had scored!! The home stands let out a joyous yell as the side referee raised his arms to signal the touchdown! JD leaped up and searched the field for penalty flags. There weren't any! His fists were in the air, pumping up and down as he was mobbed by his teammates! He had scored! The game and the bell belonged to Fort Sage!

It was a glorious moment, one that JD would long remember. The players on the bench and the home fans rushed the field. The referees, seeing that no time was left on the clock, jogged off the field, leaving the final score Fort Sage 18, Central Valley 17.

John Douglas found himself at the bottom of a huge pile of players, coaches and fans at the goal line. It got so bad that he crawled his way out and stood off to the side, unbuckled his chin strap and took off his helmet. He watched, with a giant smile on his battered face, his teammates getting hugged by almost everyone in sight. Everywhere he looked people were smiling joyously, laughing, and crying. In the midst of all this, the defeated Spartans glumly left the field, not waiting to shake the Wildcats' hands.

"Well, they aren't talking very big now are they?" asked Pete, as he, Skipper, and Ross walked over to JD. The four embraced each other, shaking hands, crying unashamedly.

"I think we finally shut them up!" said Gene as he joined the group. "Great run JD! God, what a run! Give me five, up here!" he said as he held his hand up above his head. Their ever stoic tackle, Scott, sweat and dirt stained from head to toe from playing on offense and defense all night, had been standing off to the side smiling. He walked over to JD and said simply, "Good job," as he shook his hand. The young men congratulated each other with genuine affection, all agreeing to meet for burgers after showering.

John caught a glimpse of his mom at the fence over by the bench, and started to make his way over to her. His little sister Mary ran on the field to hug him around the waist. She looked up and saw the large blood stain on his jersey front.

"Eeeewww! Your chin is bleeding!"

"My gosh, John! Are you alright?" said his mother when they met at the forty yard line. Her son's chin was bleeding, one eye blue-black. A large teardrop ran down the side of her nose.

"Sure, mom. I'm OK! In fact, I don't know when I've felt better! Just a little sore!" he said, chuckling to himself.

"Boy, John, you played great! You beat those stupid Spartans!" his little sister bubbled.

He laughed again. "Thanks, sis, the whole team did a great job tonight!" And he picked her up and gave her a big kiss.

John's mother gave him a kiss on his cheek. "I'm so proud of you. You did play great! But, I think there's somebody over by the fence you ought to go talk to. She sat with us all night."

JD heard the word 'she' and looked over to the fence to see Wendy standing alone there, leaning on the chain link gate. He raised his eyebrows at his mom.

"Well, don't just stand there. Go on! We'll see you at home later."

JD hesitated. "Oh, go on!" said his mother as she

gave him a push and then took his sister by the hand and walked off toward the parking lot.

"Mom, we're going for burgers later, OK?" he called after her.

She turned and waved, signaling that she had heard and continued walking, leaving him alone with Wendy.

For a few moments it seemed like there wasn't anyone else on the field except Wendy and him. They were an island in the middle of a sea of celebration. Players, their friends and families were all around them, slapping hands, and slowly making their way to the locker room.

"Congratulations! You played great!" said Wendy as he walked up to stand by her.

"Thanks, thanks a lot! We all played great!"

A silence ensued as both JD and Wendy stood not knowing what to say to each other.

Wendy looked up into his eyes and said thoughtfully, "I remember a time when you would have taken all the credit."

JD let out a sigh. Embarrassed he said, "Well, I was a real jerk for awhile..."

After a long silence Wendy looked searchingly at his eyes. "It was you all along, wasn't it?"

"Huh? What are you talking about?" asked JD, genuinely confused.

"Don't play games with me anymore JD. I talked to Ross yesterday and I found out you had a job. And today I drove over there to Franklin's to ask about it, and I saw that old truck. He told me you had borrowed it a couple of times to run errands. It was the same truck I saw in the park after the booths were set up. All those meetings with Mrs. Johnson, her special helper she wouldn't tell me about. . . Those Mr. Anonymous notes!" Wendy stopped, reached up and lightly touched his cheek with her right hand. She softly asked again, "It was you, wasn't it?"

JD reached up and took her hand in his, and held it by his side. He nodded his head. "Yes, it was me. With a little help of course. You're not mad at me, are you?"

"Mad? Mad? Why would I be mad?" She thought for a moment, then asked, "Why didn't you just tell me?"

He was silent before he answered. "I wanted to... I really did. I guess when I realized what a jerk I'd been to you and everyone else, I wanted to make up for it. But I wanted you to see I had changed, not just hear me say it. I thought if I walked up and said, 'Hey, I'm different now' you wouldn't have believed me. I don't know... maybe I was wrong."

He stopped and looked at her. "Wendy, I'm so sorry. I've been such an idiot. I've tried. I wanted to talk. It just seemed like everytime I tried something . . . ." He released her hand. He felt like he had blown this conversation just like all their other recent ones.

He didn't know it, but he had finally said the most important thing. Those two words, 'I'm sorry', had broken through the wall between them. He saw a tear roll down Wendy's cheek. She wiped it away with the back of her hand as she smiled up at him.

"I have noticed JD. From the beginning, even though Maria and the other girls didn't want to see it. I'm sorry to." She sniffled as another tear bubbled at her eye. "I talked with your mom tonight. She told me all about your father. That must be so hard on you!" Impulsively, she moved close to him, and they wrapped their arms around each other in a long, tender embrace.

She pulled her head back, and sniffed again. She glanced up at JD and saw the streaks of tears on his cheeks. "JD, are you OK?"

He sniffed, fighting the tears. "Yeah, I'm OK. Just thinking about my dad, the game ...and stuff...He said. . . he said he'd be back. . . . in time. . ."

Wendy turned her face up toward his, her eyes almost closed, and JD leaned down to kiss her. Just as their lips met, the lights on the field went out!

Startled, they separated.

JD laughed and said, "I guess it's time to go in!"

"Yeah, it seems so. Besides, you got blood all over my shirt! Ugh!"

They turned and walked toward the locker room, his sweaty arm draped on her shoulder, Wendy's arm around his waist. They walked on in silence, each waiting for the other to speak.

Finally, as they got to the edge of the field close to the locker room, JD stopped. He turned toward Wendy.

"Wendy, you know, I uh, I heard there is a dance tomorrow night."

"Yes, I heard something about that," Wendy replied, coyly.

"Of course, you probably already have a date, but if you don't, what would you think about going to the dance with me?" JD asked the question he had been aching to get out.

Beaming, Wendy looked up at him. "I thought you'd never ask! I already told Stan and Mark no. I had just about decided I wasn't going to go!"

Elated, JD picked her up off the ground in a big hug. They laughed and talked for another five minutes before Wendy left to go home. JD was on cloud nine as he made his way over to the locker room. He saw Mac standing there with a reporter outside the door.

Mac, seeing him approach, tried to break away from the interview and met JD just outside the locker room door. The reporter had followed and Mac turned to him and said, "You asked me why we won this game. Well, brother, you're looking at one of the reasons right there!" He pointed at JD. "You asked why I decided to run the option. Well, it was this young man's idea! Our whole team played their hearts out tonight, but this kid right here played one heck of a game!"

JD blushed under his coach's praise. He was slightly embarrassed. "Ah, coach, I had a lot of help out there! Besides, you didn't do too bad yourself!" The reporter smiled, said goodnight and wandered off. Mac put his arm around JD's shoulder.

"Thanks, John, but I meant every word. You showed me a lot this year! Made me realize a few things."

The just ended season flashed across JD's memory as he stood with his coach. He thought back to what he had been, and what he now was, the hurt he had caused, his benching, and how hard he had worked to improve himself. And he knew that Mac had really had a lot to do with it. He looked into his coach's eyes and tried to speak, but his throat strangely tightened and nothing came out. Mac looked at him briefly, knowingly, patted his shoulder pads and started to walk off.

"Coach?" JD called.

Mac turned, "Yeah?"

"Coach," JD didn't quite know how to say it. How should he thank this man that helped him turn around his life? He put out his hand. "Coach, I wanted to thank you. I sure learned a lot this season!"

Mac shook JD's hand firmly and smiled warmly. He knew what young Douglas was trying to say. "You know, Douglas, I learned a lot myself!" Then they turned and walked into the locker room amid a chorus of cheers.

CPSIA information can be obtained
at www.ICGtesting.com
Printed in the USA
LVOW10s2355280317
528836LV00021B/612/P